T0374256

The Arena

WILLIAM DAVIS

authorHOUSE®

AuthorHouse™
1663 Liberty Drive
Bloomington, IN 47403
www.authorhouse.com
Phone: 1 (800) 839-8640

© *2016 William Davis. All rights reserved.*
Cover art designed by William H. Davis, Jr.

No part of this book may be reproduced, stored in a retrieval system, or transmitted by any means without the written permission of the author.

Published by AuthorHouse 05/17/2016

ISBN: 978-1-5246-0495-0 (sc)
ISBN: 978-1-5246-0521-6 (e)

Print information available on the last page.

Any people depicted in stock imagery provided by Thinkstock are models, and such images are being used for illustrative purposes only.
Certain stock imagery © Thinkstock.

This book is printed on acid-free paper.

Because of the dynamic nature of the Internet, any web addresses or links contained in this book may have changed since publication and may no longer be valid. The views expressed in this work are solely those of the author and do not necessarily reflect the views of the publisher, and the publisher hereby disclaims any responsibility for them.

Acknowledgement

There are a great many people who, in some way, contributed their time and expertise in the creation of <u>The Arena.</u> Whether in the form of editing, proof reading, encouragement, typing or the usual forms of help a writer must have. Others offered treachery – a good heal of a boot in my face. A nice sharp knife in the back. Cruel words whispered and bizarre slanders spread. But strange as our world is I have found that as painful as these, seemingly negative inputs were, they were every bit as necessary – for me anyway – as the positive input. In a strange way I thank them ... They know who they are so they get no mention here. I must name by name several whose positive contributions were truly instrumental in this works' creation. First, three people at Lamar State College. Sally Byrd, the editor of the Lamar Expressions Book. Mrs. Byrd carefully balanced what was acceptable work – no matter how well it was written – and what crossed the lines of controversy. She allowed me to constantly push the envelope of controversy. I must thank Dr. Barbara Huval for opening my eyes to the world of literature and forever altered my view of reality. To Monteel Copple ... her kindness and inspiration affected me in ways words can't express. To Kevin, Fernando, Forrest and Greg, I thank them for their time and patience in deciphering my cryptic writing as they edited and proof read my neurotic scribbling. To Vicki Hawkins for her towering faith in God and her willingness to reach out. To my beautiful wife who, so long ago believed in me and eventually endowed me with the ability to believe in myself. And last to Our Father in Heaven for allowing me to be born in such a great State and Country.

Foreword

When I was first asked by Bill to write a forward for his upcoming book, I was speechless. My mind however raced back to a day in late 1996 when I first moved out of a prison cell and into a dormitory style environment. I had spent ten years living in a two-man cell only dreaming of the day when I could have the freedom afforded those who lived in dorms. I often wondered why those who spent many years behind bars had few of the privileges that other newer arrivals had. It seemed so odd and so unfair. The convicted felons who maintained the day-to-day operation of the facility were often those with the fewest privileges. Yet here I was during the fall of 96, finally able to live like the rest of the high-society offenders.

It would be just a few short weeks before I finally would meet my good friend Bill. He had experienced the shock and trauma of harsher environments before arriving at our unit, and simply was a ball of nerves when we first met. He will always tell others that our chance meeting changed how he viewed his entire incarceration experience, yet I am the one who was forever changed from the moment we met.

Over the course of the next decade, Bill and I developed a bond that few prisoners ever get to share. Trust and honor are precious commodities in an environment like prison. There are simply too few resources, too many provocations, and too much emotional baggage carried into institutional life. Yet in the midst of that particular concrete jungle, a precious friendship developed between Bill and I.

In the years that preceded our chance meeting, I was simply living a daily struggle with how "to do time". The sad truth is that "the time" was, in reality, doing a number on me. I would not begin to see that until interacting with Bill and his new-found attempts at becoming purposeful in life. Here I was the veteran of incarceration, having already obtained an education, working in all the best jobs on the unit, yet finding myself living without purpose and meaning each day.

As the next few years began to unfold, something inside of me changed. I will forever be in debt to the God of all creation and His work in me during this period of my life. In His own unique way, He showed me how to live through the lives of those around me. He helped me to find purpose in the pain I was feeling from years of living in a world I called my own. To say that Bill was used by God to teach me many lessons is an understatement. To say that next to my wife Melissa, Bill has been the most influential person in my life is a reality. For me the most important quality a man can have in his life is integrity. Even in the midst of his mistakes and past faults, Bill has always exhibited the greatest aspect of this quality. It has been that integrity, which has led him to challenge the status quo and the systems in place in our society. It also is this integrity that forces him to write on the most pressing issues facing those behind prison walls. He has never been one to shrink from what he knows to be "the right thing to do".

So it is with much excitement and anticipation that I point you toward this body of work as well as his future work in print. Bill has a story to tell. It is one that will not only reveal his own lessons learned, but more importantly, will work toward change in the world around us. If honesty and integrity are to mean anything in the world we live in today, then men like Bill must be heard. He along with a precious few is living life like an open book; one that is a privilege to read and be a part of.

Greg Alvis

Editor

Family Net Newsletter

Introduction

The incarcerated struggle to pass time. How a person passes their time determines what effects the strange world of prison will have on them. In many ways prison is like combat – many hours of stifling boredom punctuated by moments of intense fear, anger or madness. In many cases, the fear, anger or madness cannot be controlled. The hours of stifling boredom can be. It is a constant struggle to keep your mind busy and an active, thinking person is in an hourly contest to keep their spirits alive. One must not lose their ability to feel, but not feel too much. Think, but don't become lost in thought. Without exception, those who leave prison with their personalities improved have worked very hard at it. Few do, it's sad to say. And no one stays the same. It is the nature of incarceration to either make a personality strong or destroy it. This is another rule with no exception.

For me, education was one of the things I pursued to keep my mind busy. This I hope will show in the work that follows. Without the opportunity for positive, meaningful outlets, I would have deteriorated like so many do. In my quest for positive outlets I discovered Lamar State College. I enrolled in 1997. Two things happened there that altered my life. One, while taking a Micro-Computer application course, the writing germ – laying in me dormant for so long – was reawakened. The second thing ... I learned of the Lamar State College's annual Expression's literary contest. It was in competing in the Expression's contest that the work here in was created. Through literally years of hard work and researching past winning entries I finely learned what the judge liked and was able to write both for them – and myself.

Eventually I would become the most winning student in the Expression's 23 year history. There are several reasons for this. The main one being I worked harder than anyone else. Writing skill being relative and subjective, it was my hard work that made the difference. It was very gratifying to see hard work pay off.

Few events in my life have been so rewarding as my competing in the Expression's contest. But in prison nothing is free. To stand out is to be a target. My winning brought me great scorn from my fellow detainees and my fellow writers. If I ever expected that the world of art was free from the same petty human jealousies and envies as all other human endeavors, I no longer labor under such illusions.

But for me, pursuing writing helped to keep my mind intact in that place. Higher education can be a beautiful thing. Time incarcerated can be well spent. But the opportunity to better one's self must be available. I hope somewhere, someone with the authority will read this and take it to heart, because the people of this great state must live with the products of prison – no matter how they spent their time.

WHD

Contents

Chapter 3.   2007

SHORT STORIES

ESSAY

POETRY

Chapter 4.   2006

SHORT STORIES

ESSAY

POETRY

Chapter 5.   2005

SHORT STORIES

ESSAY

POETRY

Chapter 6.   2004

SHORT STORIES

ESSAY

POETRY

Chapter 7.   2003

SHORT STORIES

ESSAY

POETRY

Chapter 8.   2002

POETRY

Chapter 1
Limits of Restraint
1st Place - Expressions, 2009

I should have known from the start where my problem with Harold would eventually lead: a violent physical confrontation. I could have saved myself almost four years of useless frustration if I had just slugged him in the beginning. But being committed to doing things differently than I had in the past, I was determined to use our system to deal with this rogue, but this only compounded the original problem. Foolish as it was, I do not regret my efforts to use our system; I believe doing so is what separates us from the lower primates. I don't regret taking the course of action I finally took. I learned a very important lesson: sometimes our system just doesn't work. You must be prepared to consider other, less conventional alternatives. Now some will say this represents a step backward and indeed, in a way it does. But physical violence was used as it must always be: a last resort.

The details of what led to the confrontation are many and varied. The main one I suspect is that Harold is a psych patient. To be fair, I am a bit of one myself. That and being Caucasian are the only similarities we share.

As the result of a stupid argument in March of 2001, Harold and I would be at each other's throats until our final finish in December of 2004. During this time, I made several peace offerings, which were either coldly spurned or accepted (but then later forgotten). The situation finally degenerated into a protracted psychological war of attrition. Countless dirty tricks were pulled ... by both of us. I was at a major disadvantage, in that

I had a great deal to lose. Many times I would be waiting to see parole or waiting on an answer when Harold would try to provoke a fight. In turn, I (being a master of the practical joke) would do something to really piss him off. *If he attacked me,* I reasoned, *I had a chance of explaining my actions.*

And as I came up for parole every year, Harold was presented with many good opportunities to test me. But his best tries were reserved for when I was waiting on a marriage seminar, the most important event in here. If I maintained a good disciplinary record, I could attend every six months. I being happily married aggravated Harold's insecurities, so my seminars became a natural target. He tried every manner of treachery and foul play to rob me of any peace of mind he could.

Knowing myself as I do, I look back on this period with some amazement that I restrained my barbaric nature as long as I did. Often I remembered the words of Thucydides, the fifth-century-BC Greek general who said, *"Of all the manifestations of power, restraint most impresses men."* How true his words were. My *restraint* was misinterpreted by Harold, who continued to see it as *weakness* or *fear.*

Another of his favorite tactics was to try to provoke a confrontation on my commissary day. As we lived on different dorm buildings, we had different store days. It is much easier to take someone to jail with you on "their" store day. And so it was on a store day that he was able to provoke me to give him a shot at the title. It is customary to get the gatehouse officer's signature on your commissary slip. To get to the gatehouse, I had to walk past the weight machine. As I walked by the weight machine, I heard someone speak. There were several big, black inmates and one medium-sized white boy pumping iron, and one of them said, "That's him there." I looked around, and Harold had a stupid look on his face. No doubt he was slandering my good name again as he had done so often. (This was another of his favorite tactics.) *What was I this time?* I wondered. *A Klansman? A snitch? A child molester?* Loud enough for everyone at the weight machine to hear me, I said, "A *man* will speak to another man's face." I walked past and was told by the gatehouse officer to return in ten minutes.

For the hundredth time, I had already made the decision: *enough is enough.* I returned to my dorm, changed my footwear, and stretched a few muscles. Then I sat on my bunk to pray a prayer I've prayed many times in my life. *"Father, let me avoid this violence. If not, let my aim be true."* I think by the time I was on my way back to the gatehouse, I could have let the matter go had fate not intervened. As it turned out, the commissary line had formed almost all the way back to the weight machines. Further contact was inevitable.

I had some size on Harold, but I also had ten years of hard living on him as well. I had broken the fourth metacarpal of my left hand the year before. Because the bone had not been set correctly, my hand healed up partially crippled. My blinding left jab was no more. I've been into various forms of martial arts almost my entire life. Despite my tattered physical condition and advanced age, I could still take care of myself. Harold was stout and hit the iron regularly. I had once seen him pull out one of his own teeth. Not everyone can do that; I knew he didn't fear pain. And as he had made fun of the martial arts on many occasions, I intended to test his tolerance to pain (and perhaps help him with another tooth).

When I got to the end of the line another remark was made, and I basically called him out. To my surprise, he stepped out. He walked right into a front kick to his groin. He jumped back and told me, "You kick like a girl." I think he hoped to get it back on a verbal level, but that was not to be. I was already in the mode, and I had thought of this moment for way too long. I threw a leading roundhouse kick at his head, which he barely ducked. He let me get too close, and I buried the toe of my brogan first in his thigh and then in his chest. He was backed to the weight machines, where I slipped a good right cross through his defenses and landed a shot squarely on his jaw. Ah, the sound that made ... its music, I tell you! Anyway, he then grabbed me, so I thumbed him in the eye. He managed to partially dodge it before he pushed me back over the bench rest. I went all the way to the ground, but I pulled him down with me. Even though I was pinned down, I was still able to hold him in position. With my free leg, I executed a Bedinski heel smash to his forehead—twice. This move ended the conflict. By this time, people were calling out, warning about the police. As we were breaking it up, a lieutenant walked by. He looked at us like we were crazy, but he said nothing.

When I got back in line, a friend looked at me. "How did that feel?" he asked. I thought for a moment before responding. "Good," I said. "Damn good."

Harold never bothered me again. He later told me he was being harassed by a "tuffy" after learning he had made parole. Much to my surprise, he added, "I guess I got that coming."

I then asked him if he had ever heard of Thucydides.

The Interview

Expressions, 2009

The following is a special interview with President Ralpho Mbeebwee of the newly formed African country of Namgondia. Unfortunately, journalist Bob Baxter died while on assignment in that country.

Baxter: Good day, President Mbeebwee.

Mbeebwee: Boob, the only good day in Namgondia will be the day that criminal Botswana and his supporters are eliminated.

Baxter: Let's speak on that a moment, Mr. President. There are many in Namgondia who say the recent elections were rigged, and that the supporters of Dr. Botswana were—

Mbeebwee: Let me stop you there, Boob. I will not respond to questions that cast a shadow of dishonor on our legally elected government.

Baxter: Mr. President, how do you respond to the many who say behind every "Vote for Botswana" sign was a Mbeebwee henchman with a Kalashnikov assault rifle in one hand and a dead chicken in the other.

Mbeebwee: Boob, this is a ridiculous accusation. It shows how dangerous and desperate Dr. Botswana's supporters are.

Baxter: But President Mbeebwee, there is news film footage that shows what appears to be men with rifles and dead chickens.

Mbeebwee: Boob, things are not always as they seem. Some are government security forces, perhaps they are simply returning from the market. Some are Botswana supporters, perhaps placed there by your ZIA.

Baxter: President Mbeebwee, your chief critic, the renowned Dr. Charles Botswana, is in hiding. He claims a price has been put on his head. How do you respond to this charge?

Mbeebwee: Boob, Dr. Botswana has been charged with some very serious crimes. Among them sedition, treason, and conspiracy.

Baxter: Dr. Botswana predicted widespread violence should the Mbeebwee party win the election, and now—

Mbeebwee: There are attacks on government installations, the violence is on the part of the Botswana followers.

Baxter: Over one million Namgondians are refugees, fleeing the violence. Who is left to attack government installations?

Mbeebwee: Enough of this line of questioning, Boob.

Baxter: Does the Mbeebwee administration have any plans to address the unrest in your country?

Mbeebwee: What unrest, Boob?

Baxter: The one million refugees.

Mbeebwee: This is a free country, Boob, not like your America. People are free to cross borders at will. And I must remind you Boob, you are in our country now. You are subject to the laws of Namgondia. We are not afraid of America and your ZIA.

Baxter: What do you say to the charges by many who say international aid is being confiscated by government troops – that humanitarian aid only goes to your supporters?

Mbeebwee: The west made the same charges in Somalia in 1993.

Baxter: But Mr. President, there is no doubt that was happening. Also, the one million refugees, they are dying by the thousands and have received nothing ...

Mbeebwee: Boob, the refuges bring this hardship on themselves. As long as they follow that mad man Botswana there will be violence and unrest.

Baxter: Come now Mr. President, a "mad man", Dr. Botswana is a winner of the Noble Peace Prize, he is an internationally recognized figure, and he has contributed greatly to the ...

Mbeebwee: Boob, the Noble Peace Prize is nothing but a Zee.I.A. front. Just as is Amnesty International and the Red Cross. All fronts to deceive a restless population.

Baxter: Would you describe the one million Namgondian refugees as ... restless?

Mbeebwee: Boob, such remarks could damage your credibility. Journalists have a grave responsibility. When criminals like this Botswana fellow are able to trick journalist like yourself it only helps to perpetuate ferment in a restless people.

Baxter: Restless like the refugees?

Mbeebwee: Boob, if you continue to display such pro-Botswanian views you may come to discover that you have attracted the attention of the government security apparatus.

Baxter: While we are on the subject, let's talk about that a moment. Isn't it true that Director of Security Douglas Bomamba is your brother-in-law and that he is responsible for extensive human rights violations?

Mbeebwee: Boob, Doug, er ... uh ... Director Bomamba is very efficient and his position is based on his efficiency. Efficiency and loyalty, a delightful combination. Recently he was quick to subdue foreign subversives.

Baxter: By "foreign subversives" you mean a group of aid workers and German journalist Hans Muller?

Mbeebwee: Boob, this group was detained after a tip by a concerned citizen led to a search of their room. The search produced contraband. The evidence was irrefutable.

Baxter: about the evidence ...

Mbeebwee: Marijuana Boob.

Baxter: But Mr. President, you declared marijuana legal in Namgondia ...

Mbeebwee: Only for its citizens. Minister of Justice Fuso has declared its use legal, only for loyal citizens.

Baxter: President Mbeebwee, Minister of Justice Fuso, isn't he your cousin?

Mbeebwee: Boob, your line of questioning grows irritating. My patience is not inexhaustible. I have tried to answer all of your questions reasonably. I will remind you again Boob, this is not America.

Baxter: OK Mr. President, we will change the subject. What do you say about the international outrage over the death of a foreign correspondent in Namgondia?

Mbeebwee: There is nothing to comment on. Mr. Muller contracted malaria. It was an unfortunate circumstance.

Baxter: Mr. President, it is said that Hans Muller died while being detained after an interview with you.

Mbeebwee: Mr. Muller was being detained for security violations. Arms, explosives and anti-government literature was found in his hotel room.

Baxter: I thought it was marijuana ...

Mbeebwee: Arms, marijuana, does this really matter Boob? Mr. Muller had been warned as you have been, several times now, about his questions and remarks. His persistence led to other things ... and of course the marijuana.

Baxter: Mr. President, about Hans Muller's body ...

Mbeebwee: No boob, there will be no more questions. It seems there are some men here to speak with you. I hope you will have a pleasant stay here in Namgondia.

The Vineyard

1st Place – Expressions, 2009

We are bound by vines of sadness
And your pain ... is also mine,
We press the grapes of sorrow
And they yield a bitter wine

These grapes of sorrow flourish
In this vineyard that we keep,
As one, we drink this bitter wine
From this harvest that we reap

Feelings we do not understand
That have lasted through the years,
Now obscured by tangled vines
That are watered with our tears

These tears ... we cry together
And it is said by all who know,
We are tied by vines of sadness
And our tears do make them grow

So I pray to God in heaven
As I write these simple lines,
That He will stop our rain of tears
And free us from these vines.

To Joy ...

King Archituethis

Expressions, 2009

Oh King Archituethis
Ruler of the deep,
Why do you hide yourself from man?
What secrets do you keep?

In days gone past you ruled the sea
And for reasons no man knows,
The only ships allowed to pass
Were the ones your Lordship chose.

For all were subject to your rule
And you did with them as you pleased,
And men who entered your domain
You came upon and seized.

Toys for your amusement
These wooden ships of men,
And those who sailed without consent
Did not live to sail again.

But now, Oh Archituethis
You hide yourself from men,
I know that you are there oh King
And you wait to rule again.

13

Chapter 2

Group Therapy

1ˢᵗ Place – Expressions, 2008

Well, here I sit in group therapy doing a writing exercise. When I asked what I was supposed to write about, I was told, "whatever is on your mind …" Is he kidding? He can't be serious. I'm a neurotic, bi-polar manic. I suffer from delusions of grandeur … I'm paranoid … surely he jests. Or perhaps he is doing a detailed study on psychosis. Or perhaps this is a trick. . A clever ploy to see what I write. Ask me to just write what's on my mind thinking I will write something other than what is on my mind that can be analyzed, but the subtle truth is he really does want what is on my mind. Ah ha! I now have this figured out. It's a detailed study to see if, in fact, all writers are psychotic. They say all forms of genius are rooted in some form of psychosis. By those standards this could be some sort of entrance exam. I look around and these other people look no more stable than I. Look at them all. Scribbling away or sitting there scratching their heads. I doubt any of them have figured out what is going on here. They just keep writing away not realizing their thoughts will be picked apart. Come to think of it, they may be onto something. Introduce this test to all who think they need this. They could assign a certain status according to the level of psychosis one demonstrates. Actually cultivate neurotic behavior and channel it into an art. Yes, that's it. Make psychotic writing into an art form … Oh wait, I have already done that. That's what got me here.

Oh, what's that …? Write a poem? What the hell is he talking about, write a poem? I'm already writing something. Oh, I see, yes, he figured out what I am doing. Clever bastard, trying to throw me off balance. I'll not fall for this. Let's see ... Need something to pass as a poem. Anything will do. People will accept any kind of rubbish as poetry. Like time, poetry is a manmade concept ... Let's see ...

Blank Mind ...

I just used up all I had.

So here I sit, nothing left to say.

Can't be the end ... They say you can always dig deeper.

Deeper, deeper, deeper ...

Deeper still ... Isn't that how graves are dug?

There you have it, a work of art. I'll give this malarkey some fancy title. "Dig Not A Hole". Ah yes, the great work by so 'n so, "Dig Not a Hole", a deeply spiritual account of a man's descent into the innermost recesses of his soul. Ah, the critics will go crazy over it. Then, when they proclaim it a great work, I will expose them for the fools that they are. That's not a great work you imbecile, it was me killing time in some stupid therapy class. Ha, ha, what do you have to say to that, Mr. Art critic? Caught in your own trap! Dig not a hole without filling it back up, lest you fall in it! Oh, hold on ... Dig? Dig, dig, dig ... Dig deeper ... My God! "Dig Not a Hole" is a work of art. I've been tricked into creating a "something"! Who knows what obscure bits of prattle will become tomorrow's archive treasures? Hell, look at our great Constitution. It was written by a group of renegade winos, and pot heads (Actually opium-heads.) on the run from other countries. Just consider our founding fathers for a moment. Washington was a bleeding Freemason for God's sake. And how about that old fart, Ben Franklin? What an old lecher he was! And what about the Gettysburg Address? Lincoln's own words were "that will never scower ..." Scower? Scower my ass, what the hell is that supposed to mean? If that's not psychotic, what is? Genius or psychotic? But when you look closely at many of our greatest historical figures, they were just as crazy. Old' Churchill coined the phrase "Black dogs of depression". And Machiavelli? Ever read any of his crap? Prince Machiavelli? More like Prince Loon-O!

Oh, what's that? Time's up? Stop writing? Yeah, right. Now you want to silence me. Not quite the same when someone figures you out, huh? No thank you sir, I'll not be silenced. What? Disturbing the class? This group? Ha, ha! It is to laugh. The only one I'm disturbing is you. You can't stand it because I have figured you out. Thought I wouldn't catch on to your little scam, did you? Well, now you know better. Oh yeah, that's right, make a phone call. Don't dare to argue such a weak position in front of the class. Who are you calling, the C. I. A.? What are you going to tell them, I'm a subversive for talking bad about Ben Franklin? You stuffed shirts are all the same. Sit high on your pompous asses hiding behind your spectacles, then when somebody catches you in one of your games, you change the subject or ask them to write a poem. Then, when your subject refuses to give quarter, you fake a phone call. I'll bet no one is even on the other end of the line. Yeah, keep looking crazy at me while you move your lips. What a fake old bastard you are. Got to give it to him, he's faking a good phone call. Some may even fall for it. Now he has the rest of the class looking at me. I'll pay no attention. But first ... (I just thumbed my nose at that old Billy goat!) Now, where was I? Oh yes, Nietzsche. The guy that thought he could run God out of town. Died in a nut house. Well duh, why do you think they call him God? What a loser!

Ah, some new students. Must be, they are wearing white. Wherever they are from, they grow them big. Well, they seem to be working their way over here. What? Can't you see I'm writing? What, that old poof? Pay no attention to him. Just between you and me, I don't think he is all there. Do what? Escort you? What? You don't know your way around. How did you find this class room? Excuse me fellow, but if you don't give me a little room, I'm going to have a panic attack on you and your friends. Oh, is that so, you want to try? Oh yeah? That's right, spread out. How about a what? How about I shove a thumb in your eye socket, fatso? Relax? ... Relax my ass, get away from me and I will ... I'm warning you. (Thump!) How'd you like that? Hey, get that thing away from me Bozo. I tell you, I don't do needles. Ouch! Let go, you big buffoon. What wazh that shtuf ...? You shnuke baslards ... Tink I'm gonna puke ... Oooh ... Slurned th slights out ... ZZZZZZ ...

Dear John

Expressions, 2008

Jonathan Eddows Fenwick

As sheriff of Manchester Borough and Enforcing constable of Manchester proper, I am hereby exercising authority endowed me by the Queen's Crown this _____ day of 18 ____ to place under arrest and confine one Jonathan Eddows Fenwick for the murder of Thomas Skelton. You are hereby ordered to surrender yourself without parley to confinement until trial may be held.

Sheriff of Manchester Borough

Jonathan Eddows Fenwick

I trust you will hear me out, perhaps with more diligence than before. Though I doubt to expect it. Your delinquent behavior has again brought tarnish to the Fenwick name. My God, a noose fitted for a Fenwick neck, unthinkable!

Two of Manchester's finest sons dueling to the death over a peasant girl, inconceivable! I knew association with that rogue fraternity would come to no good. Still, your affiliates, I dare not call them "peers", are nothing if not loyal. That pirate O'Shea and lackey Pennington paid their respects today. Were it not for their past service to the Queen and the Fenwick family, I would have had them both arrested straight away. They and that brother of mine have set their hands to plotting. If you escape castigation it will be by their effort, not mine.

Sir Dillon Fenwick

Jonathan Fenwick

Aye Johnny, a fine kettle you're a brew'en. It's an ill wind that blows no good at all. You made an honest man of that nay-bob Skelton. Were he fool enough to cross rapiers with me lad Johnny boy, he deserves his runnin' though.

Listen Johnny boy, your Father is sore pained. Aye, the Fenwick name and all. Sore pained. But lad, you've a good many fellows who will stay the bloody end. The old God of the sea, aye Johnny boy, if he holds his wind a fine lot will watch'ya hang. If not we'll share a tankard of ale. Calm seas to ye Johnny.

Captain Dugan O'Shea

My Dear Jonathan

From the first time you held me in your arms I knew our lives were one. Your chivalry has touched my heart as nothing in life ever has. Never had I known real happiness before that day on the banks of the Mersey. You made my dreary life a thing of beauty. Now they may demand yours. Shall you see the gallows, I will look on with the alchemist phial in hand. You will not leave this earth alone my dear Jonathan. Do not protest my act of love, I could no more live without you than you could suffer the insults hurled at me by that rogue Thomas Skelton.

Your Uncle Nathan sought me out. He is a very kind man. He speaks to me as if I were a lady of high class. He wishes me to meet your Father. I fear this Jonathan, for I know your Father's feeling on this matter. I leave this to your judgment. I have so great a trust in you. I will do as you direct me. You are always in my heart. God keep you, Jonathan.

Sally Littleton

Dear Jonathan

Well dear nephew I have asserted my influence to the fullest. We must trust in the great mercy of our Lord and the wisdom of the Queen's justice. The minister's head clerk assures me he will present my petition to Lord Basil with all speed. Do not pain yourself with concern for the Fenwick family name, it has withstood more severe scandals. Your dear Sally sends her love. She is a jewel Jonathan; we must save you for her. I am trying to persuade her to go with me to meet your Father. I feel she will surely charm him as she does all who meet her. May God make you both strong.

Nathan Fenwick

Dear Jon

Here is a stroke. It seems Lord Admiral Sessions was there. It is true Jon, I read an article in the London Observer. He was in Bristol Square when you did in that dandy Skelton. Admiral Sessions paid fair report of your style. Claimed it was the best swordsmanship he had ever witnessed. This is bound to make a deal of noise. Your Uncle has taken to his heels to search this thing out. It could be a fortunate thing Jon, the Lord Admiral being an old fencing sport. He deals weightily with the ministers you know. Personal friends with Lord Basil himself, regular mates they are. I will assist in your case Jon. Make known to us your needs and we will see to them. Take care Jonathan.

Alford Pennington Esq.

Dear Jonathan

Time is short, so must this letter be as there is a great deal to see to. Sally's visit to see your Father was a smashing success. He resisted with typical Fenwick mettle. When he learned our dear Sally carries a Fenwick heir his façade crumbled. He cried on her shoulder for a quarter of an hour. Needless to say he has cast his lot with us. I must sign off. Enclosed is a partial summary of Lord Admiral Session's report to Lord Basil. I take great heart in the recent turn of events and am cautiously optimistic. God be with you Jon.

Nathan Fenwick

Lord Basil, Minister of Justice

On this _____ day, year of our Lord 18 _____, I passed through Manchester Borough to tour the spring carnival season. As my entourage passed through Bristol Square my attention was arrested by a clamor. As I approached I witnessed a contest of rapiers. This engagement had the form and fashion of a duel. I later learned the whole of the matter, the two contestants being J. Fenwick and T. Skelton. This resulted in the death of T.

Skelton. Both men demonstrated a singular agility and skill. As a guardian of England and in service to Queen Victoria, I felt a stringent obligation to make inquiries. The sum of these inquiries, outlined herein, coupled with Fenwick's actions surely dispel any allegations that this was a duel. It was clearly self-defense. Twice Fenwick executed a superb crescent de'eppe, disarming Skelton. Twice Skelton retrieved his weapon and pressed the attack. Finally after Fenwick was wounded in the arm he executed a devilish good Rook le thrust, and ran Skelton through. At what time he dropped his weapon and cried for the fallen competitor. Then he sat while the authorities were called for. Surely the weight of English honor rests with Jonathan Fenwick and the Queen's justice shall call for re-evaluation of the charge ...

Lord Admiral Sessions

Jonathan Fenwick

Aye Johnny boy, by the time you read this you'll be buried in sweet Sally's ample bosom. A hundred crown lad, is what it cost to steal me into the hearing.

Aye Johnny, worth every finning. Queen Vickie sat in as you know by now. Your Uncle Nathan presented his petition. Sly dog, were he not a barrister I'd 'ave him on me deck as first mate. Then Lord Admiral Sessions recited his summary. Aye Johnny, that nay-bob Prosecutor looked like a kicked dog. Ah but Johnny when yer dear Sally told her tale, Miss Vicki wept like a break'n wave. Aye Johnny boy, moist her eyes and even more me thinks her knickers. She waved her arms about demanding mercy for ya. Ye know how Vicki feels for our women. She ordered Lord Basil to see you released forthwit'. Ah Johnny, there'll be a wedding in Manchester soon. The old God of the sea, he's a plott'n quite a course for ya.

Captain Dugan O'Shea

Exponential Imagination

Expressions, 2008

Archimedes possessed a mind that was far ahead of his time. Modern scientists and mathematicians are amazed at his achievements, inventions and imagination. He is considered one of the three great mathematicians of all times, along with Isaac Newton and Karl Fredrick Gauss.

Archimedes was born in Syracuse Sicily, a Greek colony. The exact time of his birth is in question, but 287 B.C. is the accepted date. His father, Phidias was a noted astronomer. Archimedes was schooled at Alexandria, the world center for scientific study at the time. He was a follower of the Euclidean school of thought. His range of study was quite diverse and extensive. It included arithmetic, plane and solid geometry, mechanics, hydrostatics, optics, astronomy and astrology. He was also a prolific writer and we are fortunate indeed to have many of this extraordinary works that describe his theories and discoveries.

Archimedes' writings include, <u>Floating Bodies</u>, <u>The Sand Reckoner</u>, <u>Spirals</u>, <u>Conoids and Spheroids</u>, <u>Equilibrium of Planes</u>, and <u>Measurements of the Circle</u>. Archimedes gave the approximation of the value of Pi, ($3 - 10/70$ > Pi $3 - 10/71$). He arrived at the upper and lower bounds of Pi by starting with one hexagon that circumscribed a circle and another hexagon inscribed inside the circle. He doubled the number of sides of each hexagon until both were 96 sided figures. By this process the circle was trapped between an upper bound (circumscribed figure) and a lower bound (inscribed figure).

In <u>Spirals</u>, Archimedes defines what is known as the "Spiral of Archimedes", (ie) r = a Θ, where r and Θ are polar coordinates.

But his work <u>The Sand Reckoner</u>, is one of his endeavors that prove his imagination was beyond any of his time, and that he was thinking wholly original thoughts.

In this amazing work, Archimedes describes a system for expressing immense numbers. An example of his advanced thinking was a calculation for the number of grains of sand in the universe. He calculated there were approximately 10^{63} grains of sand in the universe. Such numbers had not been considered in Archimedes' time. He also expressed numbers as large as (10^8 x 10^8) ^{108}. This would be a one followed by 80,000 million, million zeros.

Further proof of his extraordinary mind is lost works concerned with the investigation of polyhedra (the naming of numbers), balance, levers, and the center of gravity.

Archimedes is accredited with the development of the theory of specific gravity, (ie), the ratio of the density of any substance to the density of some other substance taken as a standard – water being the standard for liquids and solids and hydrogen or air as the standard for gasses. (Also called relative density).

Archimedes invented many practical devices in his time. Among the most famous the "Archimedean Screw". He invented this while in Alexandria for irrigating fields in the Nile Valley. True to his nature, it was based on two geometric forms, the helix and the cylinder.

Legend has it that Archimedes told King Hieron, "Give me a point of support (fulcrum) and a long enough lever and I shall move the earth". When the King asked for proof, Archimedes used a system of pulleys to lift a fully loaded ship from the harbor.

About 214 B.C. his native city of Syracuse was besieged by the Roman general Marcus Claudius Marcelles. Archimedes inventions were used in defense of the city, including catapults, grappling hooks and missile launchers. In fact it is believed the Roman ballista was based on a catapult design of Archimedes.

When the city of Syracuse fell, Archimedes was absorbed in contemplation. He had drawn some geometric figures in the sand. Unaware the city had fallen to the Romans, he paid no attention to the approach of a Roman soldier. As the soldier neared, Archimedes cried out, "Disturb not my circle." At this the Roman soldier unsheathed his gladius and struck him down, so ending the life of the most extraordinary mathematician the world had yet known.

On Archimedes' tombstone was chiseled a figure of a sphere inscribed inside a cylinder and the 2:3 ratio of volume between them, the solution to the problem he considered his greatest achievement.

The Debt

Expressions, 2008

Once I was so down and out,
No friends, a complete unknown;
Empty pockets ... without hope,
And no way to make a loan.

From day to day, I did without,
My belly growled, my head hung low;
Then one day a hand extended,
But the face, I did not know.

This hand reached out to give to me,
And the face became my friend;
Because I was a man without,
He would extend his help again.

Finally, I had to speak,
For I was building quite a debt;
I asked my friend, "How can I pay?"
He answered ... "don't forget" ...

"Do not forget the needy,
The debt you owe, is not to me;
This debt is passed from man to man,
And continues on, you see" ...

"I once was ... where you are now,

And the debt began anew;
A friendly stranger passed it on,
Now, I pass it on to you."

And so my hard times ended,
The hunger pangs are long since gone;
I won't forget the debt incurred,
And will not fail to pass it on.

... Dedicated to Greg Alvis

Sand Castle

Expressions, 2008

I saw a young child building
A sand castle by the sea;
So committed to his work
That he took no note of me.

His dedication to his task
Was a wonder to the eye
Bit by bit, the castle formed
As the pile of sand grew high.

I marveled at this child I saw
The work he had at hand
It was as if he saw his future
In a million grains of sand.

And then he looked upon it
Before his work he stood
His pride did show, for the finished work
And indeed, the work was good.

Then I heard his mother call
And in a moment he was gone
But tomorrow another child will come
And the work will carry on.

Chapter 3

Divergent Views

Expressions, 2007

The following are two reviews of the latest work by play-write Chester Verimeier, entitled <u>A</u> <u>Pious Pettifogger</u>.

****

While society has rejected Chester Verimeier's first two works, it is certain his latest creation is already altering the status quo of the performing arts.

With "A Pious Pettifogger" the artful Verimeier has cast aside all restraint and produced a work so complex, so truly rich in humanistic Neo-Nihilism, no one can experience it and not admit they hold no right to occupy space in the universe.

Verimeier's critical evaluation of the social conflict between contrasting ideas can only be hailed as truly revolutionary. All of society's denizens ground under-foot will rally behind his neatly symmetrical plot, and rejoice at his extravagance of rhetoric that places rightful value on all voices that refuse to conform to <u>any</u> system of belief.

His carefully modulated abstractions highlight a flow of metaphysical sensitivity that is often rent asunder by today's harshly conservative, war mongering hatred of anything new, strange or different, illustrating the frigidity of human moral dogma.

The extremely clever introduction of the Pettifogger – a sexually dysfunctional social outcast is a splendid demonstration of the universal truth of the ultra Neo-Nihilist; that not only does nothing matter within the constraints of rational thinking, but that all ideas are composed of the same meaningless material as the universe itself.

Verimeier, in an utterly brilliant choreographing of action and contemplation, moving between specific external events and the static miasma of social containment, can only release a new and purposeful meaning in a world devoid of any real significance.

But Chester Verimeier does more than merely demonstrate the ultimate meaning behind the wasted effort of living and the nothingness of matter, he lays bare the societal stagnation – a product of latent Victorian sexual repression that has so permeated the fiber of the twentieth century. A repression that now threatens to destroy the promise of a new and fantastic nothingness that could be ours in this, twenty-first century.

Already the factions determined to believe in something – anything – are clamoring for "justice" and are decrying the work of this precocious genius. Their unreasonable protest, spreading like a wild Neisseria, demanding answers from one whose whole being is dedicated to the intricacies of metaphysical barrenness and an existential void.

Verimeier, in his majestic boldness, shows through his idealistic personification of social ills, the utter futility of life. His protagonist, Googlefritter, an unemployed circus performer with a speech impediment is robbed of his self-worth by a heartless society. He, in turn, by robbing graves and embracing the remains of others is able to find love in the only real way he has ever known.

Who are we to denounce his method of connecting? What natural law empowers us to imply he is disgusting or grotesque? What right has society to label this innovative character, unwholesome? These same voices would stamp the kindly pedophile a "sexual predator" or an enthusiastic pyromaniac a "fire bug" or a fun loving user of hydrocarbon inhalants a "glue head." What gives society the right to slander or defame <u>any</u> life style in a meaningless universe?

Such an out-moded, restrictive and useless system of belief is what Chester Verimeier has set himself to free us from. Let us pray, like groveling Christian peasants, to the great nothingness of the universe, he is at last successful.

****

An opposing view by another critic.

When I first began reading the new screen play for the performing arts production of, "A Pious Pettifogger", by Chester Verimeier, my first thought was, "they have not yet netted this morally arthritic, lecherous old mongrel?"

Then my thoughts progressed along the lines of perhaps saving the manuscript in case I run short of toilet paper. But I ultimately decided I would rather remain soiled then have any further contact with such an abomination.

As a paid critic it is, after all, my job to sometimes subject myself to work I consider unentertaining or even worthless. But wading through the cesspool of literary pond-scum produced by this perverted moron Verimeier can only be described as revolting.

Why Verimeier has not been publicly hanged, and his remains paraded through the street is a mystery to me. How anyone could find … entertaining, the exploits of a deranged, stuttering carny who gets his jollies on rotting corpses, is beyond my powers of comprehension.

It seems that since this lame bastard Verimeier has failed at his last two attempts at the further debasement of the performing arts, he is now even more determined to foul the stage. He has proven he will accept devotion from any quarter. Devil worship, sexual predators, necrophiles, militant atheist; this rabble makes Verimeier's following.

Verimeier's work, like a basket of dead voles, smells of something profoundly wrong. I would be surprised if these perversions he puts on paper were not episodes from his own life. A strange specie of being, he uses his writing to blame all the world for his failures, while at the same time broadcasting pride for his depravity.

The riot and fire at the Union Central Play House in Baltimore during a dress rehearsal of "The Rabbi Rapist" only inspired this unconscionable rogue to seek new depths with which to plunge. As one act of sickness begets another, so it was with Verimeier's second production, "An Extortionist God." The acts of public lewdness, the injuries, the indictment for violating obscenity laws and the damage to the Ralph Picasso Center in St. Louis, inspired this morally deformed little creature to produce his latest abhorrence.

If, in fact, this work is a clear indication of the direction in which literature is moving, as Mr. Verimeier claims, it is also a testament to the dangerous and widespread decay of the human character and a sign the end is near.

The Death of Freaky Johnson

Expressions, 2007

M-m-my name is M-M-Melvin Jo-ah-haba-J-Jones. Im's a cra-crack-ad-d-d-d smoker. I smokes a lot of crack. Fre-Fre-Freaky Jon-on-on-honson is my best friend. T-Together we smokes a l-l-lot of crack. Fre-Freaky, he be real sm-smart. H-He robs peoples but he-help peoples t-t-too. One day he help't an old b-bitch across de street. I know'd Fre-Freaky since we was in de gh-gh-ghetto. That be de s-s-south side of t-town. Dee north s-s-side is de rich fo-fo-fokes. It be hard to rob there Fre-Freaky say. L-l-lots of white peoples there. B-b-but even de black peoples there bees funny. One day a b-black dude sh-sh-shot at Fre-Freaky for a be-in in he yard. F-Freaky, he runs away. Freaky, he say too many white fokes gots pis-als. He say they is war-m-m-m-mongers. I tell Fre-Freaky "but you a c-carries a pis-al." He say to pr-pr-protect h-h-he self. And I says, "b-b-but you a robs folks ..." Freaky, h-he say, dem white peoples a owes us. An-and I s-say, but "F-Fr-Freaky, you a robs b-black peoples" and t-then Fre-Freaky, he go up side my head, say I think'n t-t-too much. H-he he say l-let h-h-him do de t-t-think'n. H-he right t-t-too. Fre-Freaky be real smart.

Lass Week we's a drink-n f-f-fourty ounce a-a-a 800's, on 23rd and Ra-Ra-Rosco, and we's wants some rock, but we done s-s-spent our m-money on's old a-a-a-800's. S-so-so-so-s Fre-Freaky say's, he get us m-more money. B-bout th-th-thirty minutes later he be back w-w-wiff a check. I sees it-it-it's a st-st-state check. It-its for $382 and f-f-fifty cents. It got some name, I-I-Ida D-Don-Donley on" it. I as-ax-ed Fre-Fre-Freaky, "wh-wh-who's is I-I-Ida D-D-Don-Donley?" He t-t-tells me she be some old b-b-bitch at the la-la-la-laun-washer place. S-she-she lays th-this check d-d-down and F-Fre-Freaky, he a sn-sn-snatches an-a-grabs it. S-sh-sh-she a tries t-t-to catch Fre-Freaky, but Fre-Freaky, he runs like a moe-moe, moe, moe-foe. We l-l-laughs a lot at that old b-b-bitch a-try-in to catch Fre-Freaky. Th-th-then a fu-fu-funny-ass th-th-thing a popp-ed into Fre-Fre-Freak's head. Ol I-I-Ida D-Don-Donley, he a-help't her cross de street jus a week ago. Fre-Fre-Freaky, he s-s-say that be p-p-payment re-re-received." Th-th-that Fre-Freaky, he say real smart sh-sh-shit likes that all de time. So we g-g-goes to K-k-Kim's lick-ah so's we c-c-can c-c-cash de c-c-check. K-K-Kim, he be a c-c-chin-ese or some'n. He say to Fre-Freaky, I-I-I'll a give you f-f-fifty bu-bu-bucks cus it be a b-b-bullshit c-c-check. F-F-Fre-Freaky, he go off on K-k-Kim an a say f-f-fucks you K-K-Kim an we goes. We g-g-goes to see B-B-Big Mike. B-big M-Mike, he stays on L-L-Larkin s-st-street. Fre-Fre-Freaky, he a gets $100 worth of c-c-crack for I-I-Ida D-Don-Donley's check. That s-s-shows how s-s-smart Fre-Freaky be. He g-g-ot twice times the r-r-rock for the c-c-check. We g-goes to the s-s-sand pits behind the rec-rec-rec-un yard to smokes our c-c-crack. S-s-so's we a s-s-smoken up an a drinken our f-f-fourty ou-ounce a-a-a-800's and we a sees some hoes. I waves at them an Fre-Fre-Freaky, he ax me why I do that. Fre-Freaky, he don't like no hoes cus they smokes t-t-too much. S-so Fre-Freaky he a tells me "l-l-lets hoard our rock." Hoard, that m-means lets us say we ain't got none. S-so-so th-them hoes break out a s-s-st-straight s-s-shooter an a f-fires up. Hot d-d-damn, we wills a smoke these hoes rock. I tells you my f-f-friend Fre-Fre-Freaky, he a s-s-smart moe-moe-moe-foe! So we g-gives these t-t-two hoes a f-f-fourty ou-ouncer an we really parties. N-n-now Fre-Fre-Freaky, he likes these hoes. Th-then Fre-Fre-Freaky he a tells th-these hoes how we gots the money. Cept, he says we a buys the f-f-fourty ou-ou-ouncers wiff it. We's

35

a laugh'in like moe-foes, but this one hoe (she be Desmika), she just l-l-look funny an don't laugh none. Th-th-then Desmika, she say, "y-y-yall wait here, we's go get more r-r-rock," and they's s-s-splits. I s-s-say's "damn Fre-Freaky, we has gone g-g-got us s-s-some p-p-pussy ..." We laughs an smokes more r-r-rock, b-b-buts we's hurries cus, we's a hoard'en and they be back fast. An s-s-sure as be we a-sees them a-com'n. Cept they g-g-gots some f-f-fucka with em. F-Fre-Freaky get pissed an say "we jus r-r-rob these hoes for a bring-in some fool back wiff em ..." F-F-For Fre-Freaky can a get his pis-al, th-this fucka pull a pis-al. He point his pis-al at Fre-Fre-Freaky an a say "you outta here, you theif'n m-m-moe foe ..." Fre-Freaky, he say, "if'n I-I-I stole'd, tell me w-who I done stole'd from ..." And th-this m-m-moe-m-m-moe-foe s-s-say I-I-Ida D-Don-Donley ..." He-h-he say he B-B-Biff D-Don-Donley and I-Ida be his Aunty. Th-then Fre-Freaky say, "it wont me" and h-h-he points at me. I-I don't know why Fre-Freaky do that. Th-th-then B-B-Biff say, "I jus kill boff you s-s-sorry-ass niggahs." B-bbut that hoe we call Desmika, she say "th-that fool a li-en, it be h-him who loud-moriff'n bout a s-s-steal'n I-I-Ida D-Don-Donley's c-c-check. Fre-Fre-Freaky try un pull his p-p-pis-al but th-this fool s-shoot Fre-Fre-Freaky in he gut. Th-that pis-al loud as a m-m-moe-foe. Poor ol Fre-Freaky, he bend over an a hollah, he say, "Oh's Goht, I s-sho-shot, I a di'en." The-Then ol B-Biff, he a s-s-shoot Fre-Freaky again in he knee. Fre-Freaky he fall down and B-Biff tell me, if'n I c-c-call the cops, I gets it t-t-too. P-P-Poor ol Fre-Fre-Freaky, he a bleed'n out he gut, out he mouff, out he knee and out he ass. Poor ol Fre-Freaky, he in b-b-bad shape. He a blow'n b-b-blood bubbles out he mouf. I ax Fre-Fre-Freaky why he t-t-tell B-Biff I steal I-I-Ida D-Don-Donley's c-c-check? H-h-he say some'n b-but I don't a know what it be. S-s-so I reach'd in Fre-Freaky's pocket and I gets de crack an dee pis-al an I a find some money. Why Fre-Freaky gots money. M-m-maybe Fre-Freaky a been a hoard'n dee money. Fre-Freaky say some'n, m-m-mutha some'n, I don't know what he say. H-h-he don't need no rock now. S-s-so's I takes th-the rock, the pis-al an th-the f-f-forty ouncers and I goes.

Later I a hear th-that Fre-Fre-Freaky, he die. It make me sad cus b-B-Biff, he won't even a cop or noth'en. He kill my f-f-friend Fre-Fre-Freaky. B-b-but I guess's he b-b-be pissed off cus his au-au-aunty I-I-Ida D-Don-Donley a needs her c-c-check. B-b-but I a miss ol Fre-Freaky ...

Axmehak: A Study In
Axiotransmendacitism
Expressions, 2007

Axiotransmendacitism, or Axmehak as the word was originally formulated, is a linguistic anomaly if ever there was one.

When one goes in search of this word's history they should be prepared, first off for scant information. Secondly for conflicting stories that reach as far back as ancient Babylon.

In fact, of the many dictionaries researched for this survey only a few make reference to "Axmehak", fewer still offer a definition of Axiotransmendacitism.

One, the long out of print <u>Edinburgh University Advanced College Dictionary of 1759</u>, offers this definition: "1 the use of sarcasm to pervert the truth. 2 the use of satire to confuse or baffle. 3 to compound fraud with sarcasm".

The <u>International Heritage Scottish Enlightenment Dictionary of 1770</u> definition is no more precise: "1 to indict by dubious text. 2 an invention marked by sarcasm. 3 a rude satire foisted upon the unwary".

The inception of "Axmehak" is believed by some authorities to date back to ancient Babylon. The language Akkadian offers clues to the first use of a form of this word. Babylonian legend claims the scholar Akmed coined the term "axmehak", which referred to the language the Babylonians tried to use after the builders of the Tower of Babel were confused by God.

Axmehak is roughly translated to mean, "Truth transformed into fallacy". According to Archibald Story in his out of print and impossible to find – book, <u>Questionable Stone Etchings</u>, he asserts that Akmed was stoned to death by an angry mob who misunderstood the word "axmehak" to mean, "Kill the messenger."

The next historical appearance of "axmehak" it seems was 450 B.C. in a text written by Aristippus, founder of the Cyrenaic school. He was a philosopher and historian who became obsessed with the historical origin of "axmehak". His application of "axikhiasma" was incorporated into the classic Greek language for some time.

But according to Bullard Kornberg's self-published and controversial, The Fall of Cyrene, Aristippus eventually had a nervous collapse over a suit brought against the Cyrenaic school for using a word "axikhiasma", that was deemed offensive to Athena, the goddess of wisdom. The Cyrenaic school was closed and Aristippus' "axikhiasma" was removed from the Greek language.

It seems "axikhiasma" was later revived by the philosopher Marcus Tullius Cicero in 72 B.C. The new form of axikhiasma was "axtramedatism". But like Akmed and Aristippus before him, the use of this word seemed a curse. In Roman text "axtramedatism" was translated: The use of truth to lie to a fool.

A local statesman and politician, Catiline – who just by chance was plotting against Caesar – took Cicero's interpretation as a direct ridicule of his recent speech to the senate. A political feud ensued until the death of Catiline in 62 B.C.

According to Horace Featherman's Roman Mounds, the death of Cicero a few years later brought about another change in axtramedatism. As the feud between the two statesmen had caused several embarrassing scenes, Caesar had his head scholar redefine the word to mean "a quarrelsome exchange". Its spelling was changed, again to, "conaximedatism."

Conaximedatism remained a part of the Roman language for the next four-hundred years. Then according to author and former psychiatric patient, Napoleon Bonaparte, Augustine – while bishop of Hippo in A. D. 410 – had his head scribe research the word. His scribe, Piazza Pistole, also known as the "fool of Balona", re-translated the word "conaximedation" to mean, God is a jester. Pistole was excommunicated and eventually killed.

Conaximedation does not surface again until 1540. While in a library Ignatius of Loyola discovers an essay written by none other than ... Piazza Pistole. In a final attempt to set straight the definition of "conaximedation" Ignatius commissions a church secretary to research and re-define the word. The secretary – Signore Mucho el-Mierda – gave the word its present day spelling of "Axiotransmendacitism", and defined the word to mean: Anyone who jests in the name of God will die.

Unfortunately for Signore Mucho el-Mierda, he did just that. He died a violent death at the hands of the Jesuits.

And so finally in 1801, Peter Mark Roget discovered the word, "Axiotransmendacitism". So intrigued he became with this strange word and its history, he veered away from his first love of science and medicine and became involved in a lifetime of secretary ships with several learned societies. His search led him to see a need for clarity and forcefulness of expression. For the next fifty-one years he labored, and in 1852, when he was seventy-three years old, published, <u>Roget's International Thesaurus</u>.

Historical rumor says that Roget's contemporaries – William Cullen, Alexander Primus and David Hume – all were afraid to associate with Roget as he researched "Axiotransmendacitism."

Later, Sir James Young Simson – while high on chloroform – claimed ... "Axiotransmendacitism," the greatest word ever spoken". Simson later commits suicide in prison while suffering from chloroform addiction.

Oh, a footnote on Roget's Thesaurus, it does not contain any reference to Axiotransmendacitism. In the end Roget became disillusioned with the history of the word. Perhaps sparing himself an unfortunate end. Axiotransmendacitism: a word still without a definite meaning.

Sources used:
Bonaparte, Napoleon; <u>Fool of Balona</u>
Kornberg, Bullard; <u>The Fall of Cyrene</u>
Featherman, Horace; <u>Roman Mounds</u>
Pistole, Piazza; <u>Confussa Axikhiasma</u>
Story, Archibald; <u>Questionable Stone Etchings</u>

Stalingrad: The Cauldron

1ˢᵗ Annual Publishers Award - Expressions, 2007

The battle of Stalingrad represents the apex of human suffering and waste of life in battle. The conflict that raged there on Russia's Volga River was the biggest war-related blood-letting in recorded history. From August 22, 1942 until its end in early February of 1943, Stalingrad had become a monstrous human meat-grinder. Adolph Hitler and Joseph Stalin continued to feed their soldiers to this consumer of human flesh as the world held its breath. As the carnage continued, the suffering within the city exceeded any other in history. In the case of the Russians, Stalin fed civilians to the meat grinder as well. The term "Cauldron" was adopted by the Germans and Russians alike to describe the city. The name Stalingrad became synonymous with human suffering, deprivation and the stench of death.

The casualty figures of this battle are beyond the realm of most people's comprehension. And because it was a battle that did not directly involve American or Allied forces many of the figures have not been widely publicized. Also the effects of the Cold War and the downplaying of the Soviet's contribution to the defeat of Nazi Germany has helped obscure these startling figures. The fact is that Hitler's march was stopped at Stalingrad, at a staggering cost of human life.

The loss of life and destruction of livelihood on such a scale is difficult to imagine. What drove these two armies to such levels of violence has been recorded and debated endlessly. What is less known is the aftermath in terms of human grief. The battle of Stalingrad also demonstrated the extreme cruelty of the respective commander-in-chief's. Hitler and Stalin mirrored each other in many ways. Their individual attitudes towards the expendability of human life were communicated to all the world by way of the Stalingrad stage.

Stalin refused to evacuate the civilian population of Stalingrad claiming that his soldiers would, "fight harder for a live city than a dead one." This resulted in over forty-thousand civilians killed in the first day of Luftwaffe bombing. But this was only the beginning. These corpses and thousands more would lay buried beneath tons of rubble for the next year until the official cleanup of Stalingrad began. Many of the corpses had been eaten down to skeletons by the thousands upon thousands of rats that ran wild in the destroyed city.

Likewise, Hitler's refusal to grant General Von Paulis freedom of movement, doomed the 6th Army to eventual collapse. His obstinate refusal to yield territory once captured was a tactical mistake that would cost him his entire Army. As the conflict continued, the fortunes of battle shifted many times. At one point the Germans held over nine-tenths of the western bank – the majority of the city. Stalin deliberately withheld reinforcements to prolong the battle for the purpose of surrounding the entire Army Group. As the battle continued and intensified, starvation took more and more victims. A macabre symbiosis developed between the starving people and the rat population – cannibalism by proxy. The population lived on the rats. The rats in turn lived on the corpses of the dead. Disease was rampant among those still surviving. The Russians lived off what little could be ferried across the Volga River. By October of 1942, the 6th Army was surrounded. The troops were forced to live on what could be supplied by air. An impossible task for an already over-taxed Luftwaffe. Still Hitler refused to let Von Paulis break out and consequently sealed the fate of over two hundred thousand men.

The battle of Stalingrad was the first major defeat of the German Army and a portent of what was to come. But what of the astronomical number of casualties? What of the proud 6th Army – two hundred and sixty thousand strong when it arrived in August of 1942? By January 1st, 1943, well over one hundred thousand had been killed and many more wounded – not to mention the Romanian and Hungarian troops. When the 6th Army surrendered, approximately one hundred and thirteen thousand troops laid down their arms. By the time an official count was taken a few days later, the number was reduced to ninety-thousand. Of these, fewer than five thousand would ever see Germany again. The loss of the 6th Army represented a full quarter of Hitler's men and equipment in the east – all lost.

And what of the people of Stalingrad? Most simply did not survive the battle. A census taken after the war revealed that only a few thousand of the pre-battle residents who remained in the city during the battle were still alive. Only the city of Leningrad would suffer a higher death toll among the civilian population – but over the course of a three year siege. Stalingrad took only five months. It is estimated that the Russians suffered over seven hundred thousand casualties. Over three hundred thousand of these were battle deaths. All tallied, the Russian troops, over 300,000 German soldiers who died in battle or would die in captivity. Over 200,000 Romanians, 130,000 Italians, 100,000 Hungarians, 100,000 Croatian and the over 500,000 Stalingrad civilians, and the number approaches two million.

The scale of suffering and death at Stalingrad stands as a benchmark in man's inhumanity to his fellow man and should serve as a lesson for all times. What suffering awaits a people who fail to learn the lesson of Stalingrad?

Sources Used:

Chuikov, Vasile I., The Battle for Stalingrad

Clark, Alan, Barbarossa, The Russian German Conflict, 1941 – 45

Craig, William C., Enemy at the Gate

Erickson, John, The Road to Stalingrad

Salisbury, Harrison E., The Unknown War

Missing Petals

Honorable Mention – Expressions, 2007

Such a beautiful rose,
The one that grows in the corner of the garden.
It grows by itself, away from the others.
Its crooked stem is testimony to past injuries ...
The work of clumsy, unskilled hands
That wanted only to possess this flowers awesome beauty.
But still it grows.

Some of its leaves have been dried by time,
Several petals are missing,
No doubt dislodged by an unkind gust of wind.
Yet it is the most beautiful thing in all the garden.

Surely the other flowers envy this one rose.
Ah, her thorns grow nicely!
My foolish fingers bleed, my face wet with tears ...
Shall I never pluck this beautiful rose, to have it for my very own?

(Dedicated to the Most Beautiful Rose in the Garden)

Stolen By the Wind

Expressions, 2007

We met so you could hear me out
Your ill feelings, I hope to sway
But you did not hear a single word
For they were blown away

I longed to hold you in my arms
So I tried to speak again
Just out of reach, you could not hear
The words I tried to send

My cracking voice now desperate
You must know my love is true
But as I spoke, the wind picked up
And took my words from you

Oh please wind, let my words pass
For without her, I can't live
I cried out to you louder
But the wind would not forgive

I knew that you would understand
By the power of my word
But again the wind spoke louder
And not a single one you heard

Oh please wind, do not take my words

For I must make her know
My love for her is still the same
I must beg her not to go

But as I spoke my thoughts again
Again the wind did steal
These words I tried to give you
To change the way you feel

The words did pass my begging lips
To your patient waiting ears
I can see they did not reach you
For still I see your tears

Then you turned, and walked away
Now my life is at an end
The words of love, I meant for you
Were stolen by the wind.

Chapter 4

Qutavi Bridge Incident

1st Place – Expressions, 2006

Reconnaissance confirmed that about one hundred Panthera Verde insurgents were only fifty kilometers from Qutavi, a peaceful village fifteen kilometers south of the Pena River in Southern Panama. Though lightly armed they were a threat to the village. They advanced down the El Gato Road – a decaying paved road that reached to within a few kilometers of the bridge. One battered American Dodge truck was reported to have a long tube-like piece of equipment mounted on the bed. Franco suspected a Soviet 122mm rocket launcher – a nasty concern that can "bring big smoke." To delay their advance, a small group was dispatched to destroy the bridge spanning the turbulent Pena River.

How I became a party to this rag-tag group of would-be saviors, led by a Panamanian CIA operative, was sheer coincidence. As a writer and avid river exploration freak, I was given a rare opportunity to survey a short uncharted stretch of the legendary Pena River in Southern Panama. This was set up by my publisher who had a friend in government, who had a friend at the Panamanian Embassy, who had a friend, who had a friend. I lost track of who did what. All the while I kept hearing hushed mention of the "Panthera Verde", a Marxist group committing robberies in southern Panama around the Pena River. Lately it seems their numbers had increased, as well as their crimes. Yet when I officially requested information – any Embassy warning – no one would even acknowledge there was such a group. If the

Embassy didn't acknowledge these thugs, there must not be much to them.

I was more worried about the Bushmasters that infested the jungles there. Ah, the Bushmaster: Lachesis Muta, an ornery bastard attaining lengths of over twelve feet. Lachesis has the second longest fangs in the snake world – over two inches. A bite in the field is certain death. Even with anti-venom a victim still has less than a fifty-fifty chanced of survival, and then with severe heart or nerve damage. The Panthera Verde were way down on my list of worries.

When the Panamanian River Society (P. R. S.) called and offered to sponsor my expedition, I forgot all about the Panthera Verde and their reptilian counterpart. My publisher would get a submission to read, the P. R. S. would get a report, and I would get to do what I love: float a new river, then write about it.

The Pena River is unique among rivers. Located just south of the Panama Canal, it's only actually a river when it rains enough to overflow the Pena Basin, up high in the hills. This can happen at any given hour. When it does, the Pena flows in two directions bisecting the Isthmus of Panama – West to the Golfo de Panama, east to the Caribbean Sea. For now it was calm ... for the Pena River.

I would put in (launch) at San Rabio, a small village, and with a combination of free-floating and rowing, float west to the Qutavi Bridge. I would take a few days, a week, however long I wanted. That is the beauty of "isolated free floating", all you need is a launch point, a pick-up point and a little knowledge of what lies between the two. A few tattered topographical maps furnished by the P. R. S. and interviews with some of the locals would suffice. The Qutavi Bridge was a simple, but stout heavy wooden frame supported by four twelve-inch diameter poles. It spanned the two banks – approximately thirty-five feet – and stood over twenty feet above the swift current. The only problem was the bridge was actually fifteen kilometers from the village. But, as time was not pressing I would cut a trail to the river. Easy enough because a semblance of a trail ran to within a few kilometers of the El Gato Road that led to the bridge. It took three days. Three days of ass busting to cut a trail of one and one half kilometers. The jungle seemed to regrow as I cut it.

When I first reached the American Embassy I met a fellow I would see again, Franco Valderman. I first noticed him talking to an American Marine Lieutenant. Then I saw him here and there as I prepared for my expedition. He seemed to get around a lot. I wondered about his presence until I managed to "accidentally" catch him following me as I worked on the trail I would use to return from the river. He laughed when he realized I had managed to disappear, then come up behind him. I could have laughed too, had he not brandished a Sig Sauer P-229 – 9mm pistol with blinding speed. It was this incident that broke the ice. We became friends and Franco wasn't too surprised when I suggested his Sig 9mm was "issued." But, it wasn't just the fifteen hundred dollar pistol that made me suspicious. Franco's neck and forearms – they hinted at a thousand fingertip push-ups a day. People don't maintain Olympic – level fitness to be tour guides. Of course he never admitted to anything. But surely he was some elite military hybrid. He did give me some specific information about the Panthera Verde, "meaner then 'Matas Caballo'". Spanish for "kill a horse", a reference to the potency of the Bushmaster's venom.

Franco knew of the P. R. S. sponsorship of my expedition. He finally confessed to me that keeping me from harm's way was an unofficial assignment.

"So you are agency ...?" Franco smiled, but made no reply. It was through Franco that I obtained a Ruger MK-II .22 Cal. pistol, a couple of extra magazines and one hundred rounds of old Winchester High-Speed ammunitions – just a security measure.

I had camped at the Qutavi Bridge the night after finishing the trail. I was exhausted. I had crossed the bridge after dawn to discover a stunning view from a cliff that overlooked the El Gato Road's approach from the north. Amazing, of all the jungle you could see for over a mile. I took several shots with my Nikon F-E. I had just crossed back over when I heard the sound of movement on the trail. I retrieved the Ruger MK-II from my pack and took cover behind a giant Philodendron. Minutes later I heard Franco call out.

"River Rat, its Valderman ..." I was surprised and curious. Franco and two others stepped into my campsite. All dressed in full woodland camos, all armed, and an air of urgency about them. Franco spoke in hurried Spanish so I only caught bits and pieces of what he said – something about avoiding any direct contact with the Panthera Verde. When he caught me staring at what I recognized as C-4 medium grade general-purpose explosive and #2 radio wire, he introduced me.

"This is Edwardo, my demo-man. We don't have much time." He quickly explained to me that my river trip was postponed. When he ordered another fellow to reconnoiter the North bank, I found myself speaking.

"I already have, there is this killer view ..." Franco showed a faint glint of a smile. I felt he read my mind, *"This was bound to be more fun than floating the river."*

"Davis, no American agencies are officially operating south of the Panama Canal ..." There was a certain gravity in his words. I waved him off.

"I'm not agency, I'm a rafter, besides yall are in a hurry." He nodded to another man he had just introduced as Bobby, who I recognized as the Marine Lieutenant, at the embassy.

"Lieutenant Norton – go with the good American." When we reached the cliff movement was clear in the valley below. Lieutenant Norton whispered to me,

"Pinchy Muta".

I saw what he was referring to. A fuming old Dodge pickup with a large recoilless rifle mounted on the bed.

"Simple bandits?" I asked. We hurried back to give warning. As we crossed the bridge Franco motioned for us to take cover quickly. As I looked back, my heart pounding in my ears, I saw several insurgents emerge from the woods on the North bank. All armed with Soviet AK-47's and all looking in our direction. I noticed Edwardo had connected the radio wire to a standard M-3 detonation generator. All eyes were transfixed as two insurgents stepped onto the bridge. I caught Franco's look as if to say, "*Oh well*". Suddenly one of the insurgents yelled out,

"Alambre, Alambre" (wire). Franco quickly but calmly ordered,

"Blow it." Edwardo replied with,

"Fuego en el pozo" (fire in the hold) and depressed the plunger. A bright orange flame enveloped the bridge momentarily. The bank shook violently and the air was suddenly filled with thick, black caustic tasting smoke. Bits of wood and splinters of all sizes rained down. As the reverberations of the explosion died out we became aware of the rattle of small arms fire coming from the North bank. We were well on our way, but the whiz of 7.62 rounds followed us for some time. We returned to Qutavi and the village was safe for now. Franco never mentioned any repercussions from the death of the two insurgents on the bridge.

Note: It is not the policy of the American government to conduct covert operations on foreign soil.

Any mention of American agencies or US military material, equipment, operations, or locations of such operations, are, of course fictionalized.

An Editor's Correspondence

2ⁿᵈ Place – Expressions, 2006

Editor Snodgrass; Snodgrass Publication

Enclosed you will find the first three chapters of <u>A Pleasant Summer Day</u>, a contemporary summary of life in a mid-western plains valley. Also enclosed is the customary SASE.

Sincerely, H. Binkman

*****

Dear Mr. Binkman,

I am returning your manuscript. While the writing itself is grammatically perfect, it lacks something. In fact, it is boring. You use twelve pages describing the thoughts of a single Dandelion. Not to mention the reflections of the Honey Badger. And for God's sake why does the badger think with a British accent? I don't even think the Honey Badger is indigenous to North America. Better luck next time.

E. Snodgrass

*****

Editor Snodgrass; Snodgrass Publication

I have enclosed my life's work for your consideration. I am sending the entire work because it is such a dynamic achievement. I'm sure you will recognize the truth of what I have written. Every single page of, <u>Details of the World</u> is the result of scrupulous study. I anxiously await your response.

Yours truly, G. Nerdendox

*****

Dear Mr. Nerdendox,

This letter is to inform you that I cannot return your manuscript. You failed to enclose return postage and I will not be responsible for the cost of the 3,415 pages you sent me. Also, I read very little of your work. Not only is your opening line of "In the beginning" unoriginal, but you offer no factual evidence that life began as "little wiggly things." I would suggest you condense this work and <u>always</u> enclose return postage.

E. Snodgrass

*****

Editor Snodgrass; Snodgrass Publication
Say Snodie:

Cool McCool here, say'n "Ho Ho Biddly poo, oh do I have it for you." Not since Jack Kerouac has there been a hipster like me. Me Me Me, I'll set you free. OK Snod man, here you have it. The next sensation of the nation … <u>On the Ice</u>. You can dig its' a cool, cool lit-o. Check the return, got got got you.

(Beat) Nick McCool

*****

Dear Mr. McCool,

I feel relatively certain that Jack Kerouac was not from the planet Vendicar. You, however, I suspect may be. Never have I read such, to use your own word, "kink-mikery." I'm afraid we have no need for such work. May I suggest you slow down on your drug use and seek professional help?

Sincerely, E Snodgrass

*****

Editor Snodgrass; Snodgrass Publication

Please carefully review this manuscript. It is vitally important that this work be published, that the world knows of this phenomenon. One small imbalance in the inter-dimensional time clock and we could all be thrust into an inter-dimensional transposition of cataclysmic proportions. You can exercise great wisdom in seeing this work be published.

Hopeful, Astro Zooble

*****

Dear Mr. Zooble,

I read your work with some interest. I must say, some of your technical jargon was difficult to understand. And these "others", who imparted this knowledge to you, I don't suppose they were from ...? Do you by chance know of a Mr. McCool? Anyway Mr. Zooble, I don't think that $E=V\text{-}Tm$ is for the Snodgrass Publication.

I wish you luck in your writing. Oh, and give my best regards to Zyglib should you see him again.

E. Snodgrass

*****

Editor Snodgrass; Snodgrass Publication
Heil Snodgrass,

Enclosed you will find my manuscript, <u>Actung Juden</u>. I understand you to be a very perceptive editor. Perhaps in the New World Order I can find a place for you. It won't be long either. I have great armies ... Well you will read all about it.

Zieg Heil, Adolf Hitlerheim

*****

Mr. Hitlerheim,

<u>Actung Juden</u> is quite offensive. Your ideas are disgusting. Your constant use of the term "Jewish Pig" is reprehensible. Your wish to see Israel flattened is damnable and your proclamation that everyone who does not agree with you will "die, die everybody die", is demented. I did take the liberty of forwarding your manuscript to someone who may be interested. The head of the hate crimes department at the Federal Bureau of Investigation. Have a good day Mr. Hitlerheim.

Snod

*****

Editor Snodgrass; Snodgrass Publication
Harken Infidel Snodgrass,

Allah is not without his mercy. Prove your worthiness and you will be greatly rewarded. If you show yourself to be true of heart we will accept you as a friend. Help the world see the futility of resistance. Publish, <u>The Fist of God: Death of the Blue Eyed Devil</u>, and perhaps He will withhold His mighty wrath.

Amasa Lin Baden

*****

Mr. Lin Baden,

I had our technical advisor look over the schematic of the 1 kilo-ton thermo-nuclear device that will fit into a bread box. He assures me, with some alarm that it is accurate. The long list of targets of which you intend to use this device is not only disturbing, but also monotonous. Just what do you have against ice cream vendors? Or for that matter pet stores, or ATM machines, or baseball fields, or (continued next three pages). At any rate I have forwarded your work to an interested party.

E. Snodgrass

*****

Editor Snodgrass; Snodgrass Publication
Editor Snodgrass,

Enclosed you will find my work for your consideration. I have had difficulty in finding a home for this important work. The oppression by the male member has stifled many of us truly insightful lesbians. It is time the truth be known. I hope you will take to heart the message and reply with enthusiasm.

Butchy Djike

*****

Miss Djike,

I must say, I've never read a work quite like, <u>The Prong: Scepter of Life and Death</u>. It is well written and undoubtedly you have put much work into it. I have trouble with the concept that all men should have their genitalia surgically removed. And as much of what you wrote about "improvised surgery" performed on transients is illegal, I doubt you will ever see your dream become reality. There are those who will be interested in this important work.

E. Snodgrass

*****

Editor Snodgrass; Snodgrass Publication

The timely propensities of fate have propelled my wisdomatic virtues to undertake this endeavorment of which I am strategically and immortally qualified. Choose your life's goal – thrust now or perish. This work will shock you, but if you acknowledge your black masters you will not be harshly judged.

Shaka Jabar X-man

*****

Mr. X-man,

You were correct on one point, <u>The African Fire Bomb</u> did shock me. I believe that Fredric Douglas' words to the educated Negro after the civil war were to "agitate, agitate, agitate", not "incinerate, incinerate, incinerate." Dedicated research would further reveal that the expression "honky" was not in use by the American Negro until the early 1940's. Therefore it's unlikely he advocated "burning' them honkies out." I do know someone who may "acknowledge" your work. You should be hearing from him very soon. I believe he will be quite interested in your ideas. We at Snodgrass Publication however, are not.

E. Snodgrass

*****

Editor Snodgrass; Snodgrass Publication

This is to inform you that the information you sent to this department has led to the arrest of several very dangerous individuals. On behalf of this country, I thank you. Also ... I am submitting an outline for a book I have been working on. I'm not really a writer, but I've always dreamed of trying. Just thought I would bounce the outline off you. Kind of test the waters. Anyway, thank you again from the Department and all of America.

Avery Levi, Special Agent
Liaison F. B. I. /
Dept. of Homeland Security

*****

Dear Mr. Levi,

What a pleasant surprise your letter was. I'm glad I could help in some small way. Also, your outline for your book, <u>Malignant Narcissism: A New Threat to America</u>, is the best submission I've read in a good while. Here at Snodgrass Publication we look for the informative, the suspenseful, and the interesting. Your outline promises all of this. I would be very interested in reading more. The publication of such a book could help the average citizen prepare for what lies ahead. By all means Mr. Levi, work on this and let me know if I can help in any way.

Sincerely, E. Snodgrass

The Strobe – Shopher Effect

It was the spring of 1974. The new horror film, "The Exorcist" was in its thirteenth week at the Wilshire Theater in Mesquite, Texas – the last showing of the uncut version.

This story is as much about my friend Larry as it is the disaster that followed. Larry, and most all of my friends at that time, were party animals. I prefer that term to rampant abusers of drugs and alcohol. Nonetheless, the latter term is more accurate. And of all the abusers, Larry Wayne Shopher was the most rampant. Larry had this odd idiosyncrasy ... if he was unimpaired enough to function, more dope was needed. Making a spectacle of himself and whomever he was with in public was his favorite sport. While any other "high freak" would struggle to maintain, Larry would go out of his way to see this was impossible. Not many went anywhere in public with Larry "high" more than once.

Larry showed up at my apartment that ill-fated day babbling about a surprise. He unfolded a single square of toilet paper to reveal a small blue speck. He carefully toyed with this "speck" and I realized it was many tiny blue specks. One hundred hits of "Blue Microdot" he called it. A single dose was smaller than a pinhead. He was told it was the best acid he would ever do. It was the smallest drug related thing I had ever seen.

"You're kidding me, right Larry ...?" He laughed and told me to take it, which I foolishly did. When I crunched it, I caught a slight bitter taste, not LSD ... *What then?*

"Larry, LSD is tasteless, what is this stuff?" He just carried on about how good it was. "Yeah sure, let's just go before it hits us". We had planned to ingest our party favor, drive directly to the theater, catch the 5PM showing and spare me being high on LSD and trapped in public with "head case Larry." Not to be!

My common law date had to do what women do when men are in a hurry. So we smoked a joint. Then another with a six pack. We were now over an hour late and the first effects of the "Blue Microdot" were already closing in on us when we entered the lobby of the theater.

It started out like LSD, a pleasantly stimulating, euphoric feeling of giddiness. But this had a strange numbness to it. Also a kind of throbbing in the temples. Sounds and voices had a ring to them and seemed amplified. At one point I went to the men's room. Larry followed a short time later. When he entered I was standing in front of the mirror staring at myself in wonder. My face had a mottled look to it, both flushed and blushing at the same time – a pattern of shifting colors. The pupils of my eyes were so dilated they were without color. I turned and looked at Larry and his face looked the same.

"Larry, look at yourself, look at our faces. What is this shit? We can't go out there looking like this ..." He just looked at himself and laughed. It was kind of funny. I noticed that this stuff didn't make one laugh uncontrollably as most good LSD does. And, the fact that Larry wasn't the usual clown was odd.

Then all of a sudden I became aware of the tracers. Otherwise known as the "Strobe effect", an optical illusion where a moving object is followed by a train of several or dozens of image copies trailing after. *Wow.*

Larry looked at me as I swooshed my hand back and forth in front of my face. He laughed, "Good tracers, huh?" I had never seen such vivid tracers. They were even evident in my peripheral vision. A bit of a distraction, but even more distracting was the fact that I was starting to see "floaters." Floaters: the rupture of microscopic capillaries in the neural retina and dead receptor cells in the vitreous humor that causes visual anomalies on the cornea. These appear as small fibers floating harmlessly through the plane of vision. But for one under the influence of LSD, they can appear as anything from Timothy Leary's "spirits" to Hunter S. Thompson's "bats". To me they looked like transparent snakes whipping across my field of vision.

We had lost track of time and the previous showing was turning out. We re-entered the lobby and the walls were breathing heavily. We happened to be standing by the exit aisle as a crowd of people with blank faces shuffled past. Not a word was uttered from the passing movie goers. Then I was struck by a fact: the people in the crowd had the same mottled pallor I had noticed on my own face.

From behind me someone asked, "So how was the movie?" No answer. The procession continued on in silence. Larry and I looked at each other. Slowly the entire crowd cleared and I noticed that others were watching the silent crowd pass with puzzled looks. Larry kind of laughed out, "What's with them ...?"

By the time the movie started my date was worried about me. She asked if I was okay.

"Yeah sure, why?" She thought my face looked strange. I would have been surprised if it hadn't, considering how I was feeling. Suddenly on the screen appeared the perverted statue of the Virgin Mary with its mutant bloody protrusions. I felt a deep revulsion. I turned to Larry and demanded to know what I had just seen.

He laughed and said, "Just keep watching." My date asked me if I wanted to leave. At some point I decided to watch the entire film … no matter what.

Larry got up to go to the snack bar. While he was gone the devil took full possession of the girl, flailing her around on the bed in the famous, if not revolting scene where her neck inflates. For anyone who has not experienced the loss of reality from the use of LSD, or the sickness of the uncut version of The Exorcist, description is useless. Much less experiencing these two unnatural events simultaneously. My heart was literally "in my throat" and I lost my ability to breathe for several seconds. Just as I was regaining my breath, Larry appeared. I collared him roughly and shook him accusing him of cowardice until my date and an usher made me sit.

What is the clinical definition of insanity? Who knows? I know I was very close. From that point on, watching was a tremendous struggle. The blasphemous cursing and spewing of vomit and blood insulted not just my intelligence, but my spirit. My soul sickened as the story continued. At one point I noticed an older effeminate looking fellow several seats to my right. He held a handker-chief to his mouth with white knuckles, his eyes frozen in abject terror! I was struck with a strange notion, *He is as frightened as I am.* As the horror continued I felt my soul being irrevocably scarred. I sat through the vomiting, blaspheming and senseless vile cursing, thinking it would never end.

I was distracted from this hellish onslaught by what I thought was a radio. I looked around and the fellow with the handkerchief was being helped into a wheelchair by two paramedics. I had a thought, *you bastard, you die in here and it's a one way ticket to hell* … Still, I thought him lucky, he was leaving. I turned back to the film. It finally ended. Thank God! As we filed out of the theater to the lobby, Larry's voice was the only one I heard, and I wished I couldn't hear <u>him</u>. Everyone else was dead quiet. I reflected back to seeing the earlier showing turn out and the expressions they wore. I understood then ... As we entered the light of the lobby I had a definite feeling of having escaped. Anxious faces were looking on.

"Was it good ... was it scary?" No one answered. We shuffled slowly toward the fresh air of the early spring night. Finally someone spoke up as if frustrated at our collective silence.

"Well how was it ...?" At this I stepped into the open and faced the on-looking crowd. I heard myself cry out almost at the top of my lungs, "Don't go in there if you're tripping!" I stood for several seconds exchanging glances with individuals in the crowd. It is impossible to describe what passed between us, and in remembering I ask myself if I believe it, and cannot answer. I saw several people turn and leave the theater.

Aftermath

I later learned that some wildcat chemist was producing STP, a drug several times more potent than LSD, and selling it as "Blue Microdot." I read in the Dallas Times Herald that an Albert Wriggle suffered a stroke during the last uncut showing of The Exorcist at the Wilshire Theater. He later died at Parkland Hospital. Larry finally drove himself into the gutter with his incessant drug abuse. The last I heard he was in therapy. It took me over a year to come to grips with that experience and I am still occasionally haunted by the events of that day.

Man's Wild Heart

Honorable Mention – Expressions, 2006

The American Revolution was an inevitability waiting to happen. The economic and political scene made revolution unavoidable, even more so, the spirit of the colonists.

History tells us that independence from Great Britain was the motive of only a small minority of the colonists when the war started. This is probable, at least on a conscious level. As long as the colonists considered themselves subjects of the British Crown the only source of conflict was the economic sanctions placed on them by London.

However, something more was at play within the hearts of a new generation. We can only speculate on the spirits of the colonists. But the difference in mentality from the native-born colonists and their counterparts in jolly old England must have been drastic. The wild land itself must have had profound effects on the colonists.

As new generations were born and reached maturity in this new country, they became even further removed from the British Empire ideologically.

There was no way to maintain more than a minority of loyal British subjects in the New World. And so, a shift in ideology was certain. The many acts passed in London's attempts to bring the colonists into submission were merely treating the symptoms of a much larger issue; the issue of man's wild heart.

How could you live in a land totally new to the world without such a heart? To even consider the courage and spirit of a people who would spend six to eight weeks on a wooden boat to get here makes one wonder. The people who came here and those later born here were hopelessly removed from England's civilized society – Not just geographically, but spiritually.

Once the decision to resist had been made, the British government was helpless to stop the revolution. The logistics of keeping enough forces in place to contain the movement was beyond the technology of the day. By 1775 the number of colonists were such that they could have carried on the fight indefinitely. With every battle their resolve increased. As with the first engagements at Lexington and at Concord show, the colonists had some major advantages. The knowledge of the land coupled with a guerrilla form of attack was more than the British could effectively stifle.

The spirit of the extraordinary people who shaped this fantastic new land made revolt inevitable – The unstoppable wild heart beating within the breast of the American people. A wild heart that still beats today.

Custer
An Expedient Sacrifice

Expressions, 2006

The history of our great country is replete with political intrigue. Conspiracy theories have abounded through the years. Of course, only since the age of mass media, investigative journalism and reporters who doggedly pursue any lead, has any theory caused much controversy. Deep inquiry of these controversies often raise as many questions as they answer. The nature of an investigation – if not impeded by outside influences – is final closure. Enough facts are finally discovered to give a general description of how an act was carried out and a possible motive. When any investigation or inquiry raises more questions than it answers, a conspiracy can be reasonably inferred.

One such case – where few questions have even been asked – is that of General George Armstrong Custer and his demise at the Battle of the Little Big Horn. The most commonly known version of this "wild west" story is that an over confident Custer was simply outnumbered and overwhelmed by the combined forces of the Lakota Cheyenne and Arapaho warriors. However, if one researches this fascinating story, you are soon faced with unanswered questions. Seldom is any controversial act carried out without leaving trace evidence. The same is true of the Battle of the Little Big Horn and you soon realize it shares many unsettling features with more modern conspiracy theories.

The nature of intrigue is that it obscures facts leaving unanswered questions. Questions that must never be answered if the cover up is to remain intact. So let us examine the "facts" as best we can from our chronological proximity.

George A. Custer graduated from West Point at the bottom of his class in 1861. There he earned excessive demerits and stayed close to expulsion the entire four years he attended. Custer distinguished himself in the Civil War and was the second youngest general at its end. Custer's recklessness earned him a reputation for bravery. It also earned him the scorn of many who blamed his foolhardiness for high losses among his men.

But it is during the Indian wars that troubling questions begin to accumulate. In 1876, Heister Clyman, Chairman of the House Committee on Military Expenditures, conducted an investigation into the dealings of Secretary William W. Belknap. All who took part in these proceedings acknowledge that Custer's testimony was hearsay. Despite this unusual aspect, it seems that Custer's testimony was damning. Not just against Belknap, but his testimony also implicated Orville Grant, president Ulysses S. Grant's brother.

Grant had Custer relieved of command and arrested. A short time later Custer was reinstated as Commander of the 7th Cavalry. On May 17th, 1876, the 7th Cavalry totaling eleven hundred men left For Lincoln headed for an appointment with fate.

Here the questions veer sharply into the unanswerable. First, over three quarters of the 7th Cavalry did not even take part in the Battle of the Little Big Horn. Various (somewhat dubious) ad hoc explanations for this exist. None make much sense.

But there are even more troubling questions for which there are no answers at all: where did the approximately five-hundred repeating rifles the Lakota Cheyenne used come from? The question posed by these rifles and the thousands of rounds of ammunition these hostile, non-treaty warriors possessed is one for which no reasonable explanation exists. The odor of something amiss increases as we examine the history of these rifles.

Among the repeating rifles used against General Custer's 7th Cavalry were two hundred Henry rifles and two hundred Winchester model 1866's. The Henry rifle was the creation of Ben Tyler Henry in 1860. While the Henry rifle saw some action in the War Between the States, its cost was prohibitive. At $52.50 each, it was worth several months' pay for the average man. B. T. Henry went broke and sold his company to Oliver Winchester. Winchester produced an improved version in 1866. Approximately 14,000 Henry rifles were produced. Ordinance Department records show that the U. S. Government purchased 1,731. The serial numbers are in a narrow range from 3,000 to 4,200, some 531 not listed. There is also an unexplained overlapping of serial numbers with the last Henry rifles produced and the first Winchester 1866 models. Ordinance records in the Washington, D. C. Archive's list the serial numbers ranging from 1392 to 3956, noted on a purchase made December 30, 1863. The National Archives show that 1,544 Henry rifles were purchased. A discrepancy of about two hundred rifles. The overlapping serial numbers for the first Winchester rifles produced are not available. I suspect their identification would shed light on the subject. There are several dozen Henry rifles in private collections bearing the suspect serial numbers. Most can be traced back to purchases made at Bureau of Indian Affairs auctions.

We also know the Bureau of Indian Affairs had full time scouts tracking the hostile, non-treaty tribes. Much of the time these scouts did not know the location of the tribes. The argument that "gun runners" furnished the five hundred repeating rifles is stretched beyond believability in view of this and other facts. Earlier there was money to be made by selling guns and whisky to the Indians. The fungible commodity used by the hostile tribes was gold and animal furs. By the 1870's the fur trade had dropped off sharply and the Indians were even more likely than whites to mistake iron pyrite (fool's gold) for the real thing. Aside from the fact that any kind of unauthorized trading with hostile non-treaty tribes was a hanging offense, it is difficult to believe that many freelance traders had the resources to range over thousands of square miles with dozens of wagons seeking to trade with Indians that professional trackers often could not find.

The Bureau of Indian Affairs had, without doubt, the best scouts and the most uninterrupted communication with the non-treaty tribes. This fact coupled with the bewildering question of how the most technically advanced weapon of the day found its way into the hands of the hostile, non-treaty warriors in such numbers is indeed unsettling.

Another suspicious aspect of this story is that George Custer was doing research on the Arapaho, Sioux and Lakota Cheyenne tribes and requesting reports relating to Indian agents and certain possible conflicts of interest. Ironically these same tribes would annihilate General George Armstrong Custer and two hundred seventy seven men on July 25, 1876.

History has faithfully recorded the American people's reaction to the Battle of the Little Big Horn. The sympathy that had been mounting for the Plains Indians was swept away by a national cry for revenge. Yet the actions of Major Marcus Reno and Captain Fredrick Benteen – the two commanders who abandoned General Custer at the critical moment – were never questioned. Perhaps if this and other questions had been asked the prevailing story of this incident would be different. Questions such as:

- Who had reason to want to see General Custer discredited or otherwise nullified?
- Who had the most constant contact with the hostile, non-treaty tribes?

- Who had access to the most technically advanced weapon of the day, and the resources to move them at will?
- Why was there never an inquiry into the actions of Major Marcus Reno and Captain Frederick Benteen?
- Why do none of the Ordinance Department records, U. S. Government purchase records, or National Archive records list all the Henry rifles' serial numbers?
- And last, what questions was George Custer asking about the Bureau of Indian Affairs?

All these questions point to the Federal government, the Bureau of Indian Affairs and the Grand Administration.

- Conclusion -

In answer to the death of General Custer was an era of unrestricted slaughter of the Plains Indians and within a few years, a decade long struggle would come to a bloody end. The complete subjugating of the American natives was accomplished and few would ever question the death of General George Armstrong Custer.

- Sources Used -
Adams, Linda, Emory Hackman; The Henry Rifle
Graham, W. A.; The Custer Myth
Perrett, Bryon: Last Stands
Wert, Jeffery D.; The Controversial Life of George Armstrong Custer

*****

Washington D. C. National Archive, Ordinance Records; December 30, 1863

Burn No More

1st Place – Expressions, 2006

As I watch the falling star blaze a path
Lighting up the cold winter sky

                                                    I burn …

As I watch the sun drop behind the tree line
On the horizon, fading from view

                                                    I burn …

As I see the drought of summer slowly dry
The tender leaves

                                                    I burn …

As I recall the passions of my youth in
Hopeless longing

                                                    I burn …

As the hatred boils within me for wrongs
Done I cannot change

                                                    I burn …

As they tie me to this stake for statements
Made, I will not retract

                                                    I burn …

As the cooling rain of death gives peace to
My tormented soul

                                                I burn no more.

The Vixen

2nd Place – Expressions, 2006

You frolic in the warm water
Building strength
You dance above the gulf
Keeping us wondering
You have the smell of sea about you
Your cool breeze turns violent
Then, like some woman scorned
You pound our beaches
Thrash our city
Splinter hundred-year old oak trees
Razing our homes,
Making rubble of our work
You leave women and children homeless,
Then you pass from sight ...
Leaving us to ponder our wreckage.
But the savage vixen you were ...
We will remember you Rita.

Lady Luck

3rd Place – Expressions, 2006

When I was young, I stood at shore,
Looking out to sea;
I saw a captain on his ship,
And I wished that I were he.

And as I grew into a man,
I came to know what I must do;
Learn to sail, build a ship,
And launch into the blue.

Three years of working night and day,
And then ... the champagne bottle struck;
The words still ringing in my ears,
"I christen you, 'Lady Luck".

And so the day, it finally came,
For me to leave the land;
I walked onto my Lady's deck,
And proudly took command.

I left my friends and family,
As I put my ship to sea;
I saw the shore grow distant,
Not knowing what would be ...

At night I saw a million stars,

I had never been so free;
I understood why men build ships,
And the call to sail the sea.

But one night the sea turned rough,
My Lady thrashed about;
I heard the crack of timber,
And my heart was filled with doubt.

Then lightning struck my Lady's mast,
And sent it crashing through her deck;
I could feel my Lady's pain,
As she became a wreck.

I remembered the star filled nights,
And the freedom sailing gave;
I did not regret having put to sea,
As I went to my watery grave.

Then I felt sunlight on my face,
As I lay there in the sand;
I awoke by the wreck of my "Lady Luck",
On the beach of a foreign land.

Now I have an island woman,
Suntanned breasts and a beautiful smile;
Material is hard to come by ...
It seems I will stay a while.

The fishing is good, the fruit grows wild,
And my woman likes to play;

Work on the Lady is going slow,
I might even have to stay.

But late at night I still remember,
When the bolt of lightning struck;
And how I was spared to sail again,
Saved ... by my "Lady Luck".

The Coming Storm

Honorable Mention – Expressions, 2006

Had I seen the coming storm
I would have sought a place to hide
The forecast spoke of coming storms,
But these warnings I denied

I refused to see the changing,
Because I am a stubborn man
And now the storm has caught me out
I must take shelter where I can

I shelter with the lonely
As the rain falls from my eyes
I feel the lightning strike my heart
As I recall her lies

Thunder pounds inside my chest
As I long for the love we had
Now she is gone and I am alone,
So I shelter with the sad

All the broken hearted fools
Who like me, are left in pain
Remembering a time when life was good,
Before it began to rain

I stand here in hopeless wonder

How long can this storm last?
It seems there is no end in sight
As my mind relives the past

And so the sky, it finally cleared
And for me the rain is gone
But many are not so lucky
For them the storm goes on

Now I am in love again
The sun, it shines so bright
I love her and she loves me
Not a single cloud in sight

And what is that the forecast says,
The threat of a coming storm?
I stand here with her laughing
As I watch the tempest form.

Chapter 5

A Shameful Killing

1ˢᵗ Place – Expressions, 2005
(2009 – Honorable Mention w/Pen American)

Charlie checked the Jiffy Mart from the phone booth. Old Leonard would be closing soon. He tried to imagine the look on the old man's face when he saw the gun.

He pulled the pistol from his pocket and looked at it again. A .38 caliber. He didn't know the make or model. All he knew was when he had it he was a big man.

Charlie had suffered from "little man's complex" all his life. He wasn't really small enough to have a complex, he just did. He had tried being a bully, but that had gotten him beaten up several times. Still, he never lost an opportunity to prove to himself that he was tough, or smart, or fast or any number of things he wasn't.

When Charlie had paroled the first time he was sure people would respect him because of his tattoos. He acted as he did before, people responded as they had before. When he paroled the second time, with more tattoos, he was even surer people would respect him. Surely someone of his experience was to be respected. Charlie was dumbfounded to learn that children and little old ladies were the only ones who showed something even close to what he considered respect. Of course after Charlie's early childhood and first twenty years of adult life, his thinking was so distorted that he could no longer grasp what real respect was. The concept of fear and respect were hopelessly confused in his mind. Was it the abuse he suffered at the hands of the aunt who raised him? Was it something from prison? No one knew. Charlie had driven away every friend that he had ever had. Everyone made him feel like a no-body. He noticed movement at the Jiffy Mart. A customer leaving. It was time and soon old Leonard would know he was somebody.

He told himself that if the old man made one smart ass remark he would shoot him on the spot. The old man had already shown a marked lack of respect. Leonard had no right to be as cocky as he was. Why he was hardly bigger then Charlie and had to be sixty. Like the day he had ejected the shoplifters. That old cuss actually slapped one of them upside the head. *"If he had done me like that ..."* Charlie's thoughts trailed off as he felt apprehension swell up inside. "I'm not afraid of that old fucker." He realized he said this aloud. He looked at the revolver again. Time to do it.

The isolated location of the Jiffy Mart seemed to make it an ideal mark. The fact that his residence was only two miles away didn't seem to be an obstacle to his plan for quick money. Those who do not learn from their mistakes are bound to repeat them.

As Charlie neared the entrance of the store, he noticed the old man had removed his shirt. In his tank top style undershirt his numerous tattoos were visible. *So this was why the old man always wore long sleeves.* He found himself stopped at the front door. Then his heart skipped a beat as the old man turned and looked directly at him. Seconds passed. The old coot just stared. Then he turned away and returned to the mundane task of closing up. Charlie pushed ever so lightly on the door. The bolt rattled in its housing. The door was locked. He felt relief. Then he cussed the old man under his breath. *"You're a lucky old fucker, Leonard. I'd of ..."* He stood there looking at the road and thought of his leaking frame house only two miles away. He fumed at his inheritance. He should have been given more land. Instead, he was given only a few acres and that shack. His brother, Wayne had always been favored, he had ... Charlie was startled by a rattling. Before he could snap to old Leonard was standing there asking, "you need something kid?" He stood frozen staring at the old man. "Well sonny, if you need something you better say something cus I'm closing ..."

"That old smart-ass, I ought 'a ..." His thoughts confused. More time passed.

"I'm forty-one ... old man." There, he had spoken defiantly; he wasn't afraid of Leonard. The old man's eyes squinted producing a deep set of crow's feet at each temple.

"Listen son, I don't give a good fuck how old you are. You either gonna buy something and damn fast, or I'm lockin the door." The old man's stare intensified.

"Uh, yeah, uh ... some beer." Charlie stood frozen. Old Leonard looked him up and down, his eyes stopping for a moment at the bulge in his jacket pocket. He knew. Somehow this old man knew.

Leonard stepped back and held the door. "Well I don't deliver, hurry your ass up." Charlie stepped in as if walking through a minefield. He walked to the cooler, retrieved a six pack not noticing the brand. His mind was racing. As he set the six pack on the counter the old man leaned over and asked, "Just what the fuck are you up to sonny boy. What's this supposed to be, a god damn stick up?" Charlie was caught completely off guard. As he reached his hand into his pocket the old man held up a hand.

"Before you pull that piece, let me tell you something Charlie. I don't intend to give you a fuck'en dime. As long as you don't show me that, whatever it is you got stashed in your jacket, I can sell you this six pack of friggen soda you call beer and forget this. But you pull a goddamn gun on me and I swear I'll make you kill me.

There ain't a chance in hell you'll get away with this. So make up your mind. And do it now sonny boy." Charlie was trembling so hard he couldn't conceal it. At that moment car lights flooded the store entrance.

As if things weren't bad enough, a law man. A dammed county lawman. A big lumbering uniformed officer exited the car, pushed on the front door and asked, "You still open Leonard?" He shot a cold stare at Charlie. "Yeah flat foot, may as well, I'm wait'n on this snot-nose kid already." Charlie laid a five dollar bill on the counter. The big officer stopped for a moment. "Everything okay Leonard?"

"No, hell no, everything ain't okay, it's ten minutes after midnight and I got a fat-ass cop and snot-nose punk still mill'n around. Ya'll got one minute and I lock ya'll up in here." Charlie hurried out without collecting his change. The big officer set a big bag of chips and a candy bar on the counter. He watched Charlie until he was out of sight. "That guy is trouble." Leonard met the big officer's stare. "Was a time they said that about me." The big officer laughed out loud. "Hell Leonard, you were trouble. Aint that old Minnie Preston's nephew?" Leonard looked up and answered, "Don't know, and don't care." With the big guys sense of humor completely dampened he paid for his chips and left, grumbling under his breath.

The door came almost off its hinges. Not because Charlie was a powerful kicker, but because it was so old and dilapidated. The mutt that he had been abusing for the last two months ran for the couch. After scurrying under the couch she poked her snout out looking up at her master as only a loyal dog can do. "That old bastard!"

Charlie felt as if his brain would explode with rage. "That old fucker called the cops, I know he did ..." He kicked at the coffee table sending it flying through the air. He flung the six pack of grape soda he had mistaken for beer against the wall. He leaned over and called to the mutt. She came hugging the floor, tail between her legs. Charlie looked down at the dog. Seeing something of himself in the quivering mass he again lashed out, burying the toe of his boot into the dog's ribs. The force sent the mutt into the corner with several broken. It was then Charlie noticed the small mound in the floor.

"You shit in the floor again ..." The mutt was trying to get to her feet when Charlie pulled the revolver from his jacket pocket. In a complete rage now he leveled the front sight on the dog. "Die you bitch!" One shot, a second, a third. Six in all, the shots echoing in the darkness.

The first round knocking a tuft of fur from the mutts hip, the force spinning the animal around. The exiting bullet splattering the water stained sheet rock with blood as it penetrated the clap board sheathing. The second round clipped the dog's foreleg, almost severing it. The third hitting low in the rib cage glancing down through the stomach spilling intestinal fluid out in a stream. The fourth round struck the floor well in front of the animal sending splinters into the air. The fifth round struck the shoulder at a sharp angle, slashing open a six-inch gap, then glancing away. The mutt lay bleeding profusely. Charlie then kicked at the bleeding, whimpering animal.

Leonard opened the store at 7:00am as he had done for years. He had just opened the front door when the big county officer pulled up. He again lumbered his way into the Jiffy Mart. "Say Leonard, did you hear about Minnie Preston's nephew? Charlie something ...? He tore up the old house that Minnie left him, then blew his brains out. Shot the dog, too." Leonard didn't acknowledge.

"Hell Leonard that could have been you. They placed the time of death about 1:00am. A constable thought he heard a shot." Leonard looked up with his usual cold stare. "Shot the dog huh? Shameful Killing."

Extreme Communication

2nd Place – Expressions, 2005

Matthew tried to hear Master Kim's words. Tried to feel as he felt in Master Kim's presence. *"Never react out of fear or anger ..."* But this was not an exercise in the dojo. This was not a controlled engagement, it was for real. These were real thugs. Street hoods, not his fellow students acting as aggressors. The one facing him now outweighed him by, what ... thirty pounds?? And there was the knife.

He made a conscious effort to control his breathing. As he did a fact came into sharp focus. He had never tested his martial skills under real conditions. He thought of the upcoming test for his black belt. He had been assured by many that to earn a black belt from Master Kim Jong he would get bruised - several times.

As apprehensive as he was about facing the master in a real fight, this was different. Much different. Matthew remembered his green belt. Master Kim had promised him, *"One of my green belts fight good. Very good."* He had one eye almost closed and a near dislocated wrist as a result of his green belt test - not to mention how he hurt after earning his brown belt. He wondered at his anxiety over this fellow facing him now. When once a fellow student ask Master Kim about what to do in such a situation he answered, *"give as much consideration as time will allow."*

The sound of the fellow asking something about money while brandishing the knife barely registered as he tried to follow Master Kim's instructions. *Consider ... as much as time allows.* He noticed his adversary had a weak chin. He was also missing a tooth. He stood slouching as if his back hurt. The other

88

fellow – about his size – looked nervous, as if he had had too much coffee. Matthew remembered the multiple attacker exercise: *address the most immediate threat first.* This would be the big guy with the knife, who was repeating his demand for payment. From the back of his mind Master Kim spoke, *"honest words transcend evil intentions"* ... Matt found his voice, "I'll not give you anything. I am well prepared to defend myself." Matt stepped back into an open stance. There was silence.

The big guy had a puzzled look on his face. He looked to his left to ask his cohort if he had heard correctly. Matt noticed he had taken his eyes completely off him. A show of disrespect to a martial artist, a fatal mistake in a street fight.

Matt had an urge to fire a front kick into his groin. Then he heard Master Kim again, *"Ah Matt-u, Thucydides say' of all manifestations of power, restraint impresses men most."* And while Matt doubted this fellow had even heard of Thucydides, he realized his breathing had slowed considerably. He also imagined how this fellow lost his tooth. Matt noticed movement as the smaller of the two stepped away. It was then he noticed the guy was armed with a length of pipe. So they were both armed. This perhaps changed things.

He was aware of the big guy speaking again, this time the words "fuck you up" registered loud and clear. As if almost by cue he heard Master Kim, *"confidence and courage far out-weigh cowardly boasting."*

As if he was hearing someone else say it Matt heard himself answer, "try it you big buffoon, see what happens".

The big guy took a step towards Matt. He responded by assuming a Kwon Boxing stance. The big guy stopped at what he thought was a safe distance. Holding the knife out trying to threaten, he snidely remarked, "You think you Kung Fu or some'n".

Matt noticed a slight trembling of the knife. He saw doubt in the big man's eyes.

"Ah Matt-u eyes, window of soul."

Matt's words seem to come from inside. "I am a student of Master Kim Jong."

The big guy again looked at his partner in crime. "Ain't that the gook who fucked big Burnie up?"

Before he could answer Matt found himself speaking. "Mr. Jong is a master of Korean martial arts, he is an honorable man. I advise you to speak respectfully or I'll ..."

The big guy was taken back by the fact that Matt had closed the distance between them. In an overreaction to this he stepped back, stumbling backward as he did.

The big guy's question sparked Matthew's memory. A newspaper article, *"Would be Rapist Hospitalized by Local Martial Arts Instructor."* In fact it was this story that brought Matthew to Master Kim Jong's, Hwa Rang Do studio. He remembered how impressed he had been with the witnesses' descriptions of the confrontation. He also remembered how repulsed he had been by the character of the big Burnie fellow.

Burnus Hargrove, ex-heavy weight boxer, three-time loser, drug attic, sex offender. One of those who seem to continually fall through the cracks. Mr. Hargrove's luck ran out when he put his hands on young Linda Jong. Had big Burnie not been high on PCP, it's likely that Master Kim would not have broken an arm ... dislocated his shoulder ... smashed a knee cap ... gouged out an eye ... and fractured his skull. But the big man couldn't get enough.

Matt was brought from his memories by the smaller guy's voice, "Say Spike, lets don't mess with this Jap hocus pocus - its bad man". The big guy looked from Matt, to his cohort, back to

Matt, his uncertainty was painfully obvious. The Master's words again came to Matthew. *"Always remember Matt-u, an attacker must win, the vanquished must only survive."* Could he avoid this confrontation? His martial arts philosophy required him to do so if possible. He knew Master Jong would not accept an insult as an excuse for fighting. *"Matt-u, Hwa Rang Do code, better to accept insult than risk danger, better to risk danger, than injury, better to injure than to maim, better to maim than to kill, better to kill than to be killed. Each man must decide for himself ..."*

The master's words were cut short.

The big guy stepped forward, teeth clinched. In one fluid motion Matt fired a front kick into the big man's groin. The big guy bent at the waist as if suddenly violently ill and vomiting. His knife wielding arm extended, was an easy mark. Over and back. The knife rattled as it hit the pavement.

As if in slow motion the smaller of the two raised the length of pipe over his head. Matt felt the side kick start in his shoulders, the motion traveling through his body, his hips picking up the momentum, his left leg firing out. Textbook in its execution, the extension was perfect. He was barely aware of the resistance offered by the guy's solar plexus. The kick lifted his attacker off his feet sending him several yards through the air. He landed squarely on his back struggling to regain his breathing.

Matt stood there. He heard Master Kim's voice, "Matt-u, had you good cause to risk such danger ..." He was startled. This time the voice was real. He turned to see Master Kim standing a few feet behind him.

He assumed the respect-stance, bowed at the waist. "Sensi." Master Kim bowed slightly in response. "Forgive me Sensi, after all your teaching I allowed myself to react out of anger."

Master Kim looked into Matthew's eyes and without his lips moving he clearly heard his words, *"Ah Matt-u, sticks and stones ..."*

Matthew's bottom jaw dropped. He realized the old legend of a Hwa Rang Do master, being able to project his thought telepathically was fact. All he could do was utter, "Master Kim ..."

Master Kim smiled. "Come Matt-u, you have much to learn." The moment was broken by the sudden moaning of the big buy suffering from his dislocated shoulder.

Matthew looked around and asked, "Master Kim, what about them"?

"Ah Matt-u, they have much to learn as well ..."

Letters and Dispatches

3rd Place – Expressions, 2005

TO: Sarah Ann McMillan   FROM: Lt. Andrew
                                     McMillan

      P. O. Box 100, Rt. 1   MAC - SOG, 2nd
                                     Battalion.

      Barns City, Iowa   Ranger Co. 123, Attc.
                                     24th

                                     Mech. Infantry Division

Baghdad, Iraq

Dear Sarah:

I love and miss you Darling. I'm sure you know by now that not only did I survive the snake bite, but it got me two weeks off duty. Thing about those saw-scaled vipers, the bite is subject to infection after most other wounds heal. But the free-bee is over soon. Just as well, I'm getting antsy in this infirmary. The photos of little Andy did my heart good. So he learned to walk already? Hopefully this freeze on tour rotation will end soon. Sarah, give my love to all. I have looked at the photo of you and little Andy every day for the last two weeks. I love you Sarah. God Bless.

                                             Andy

___

TO: Lt. Andrew McMillan   FROM: Art McMillan
        P. O. Box 100 ...   P. O. Box 100 ...

Dear Andy:

You don't know how relieved your Mother was to learn how prepared you Rangers are. She was also hoping the snake bite would get you sent home. She and Sarah talked about it for a week. They both suffer every day Andy. It reminds me of Nam. Only there it was bamboo vipers and Kraits. Those damned Kraits. Don't know of one victim of a Krait's bite to survive. Fortunately you're working under different conditions. Still, the lack of cover has got to be hell for recon. The corn crop is looking good. May apply for that government subsidy if they pass it. Your Father would be proud of you Andy. Just keep your head down and watch out for saw scales. Maybe you can get another two weeks off. Now I sound like your Mother.

    Stay safe Andy, and God Bless.

                                    Art

TO: Sarah Ann McMillan   FROM: Lt. Andrew
        P. O. Box 100 ...   McMillan
                                MAC – SOG ...

Dear Sarah:

Sorry it's been so long since I've written. Things have been a little hectic. I love and miss you and our son. I don't know if the news covered the ambush or not. They are getting so common. Bob was killed. So was Rich. Franklin will probably lose a leg. A lot of civilians were killed. It was a mess. There is talk that Command One had been warned. Second platoon is still out of contact. We are worried. I hate telling you this, but we promised ...

Sarah, I need to write Mr. Hammons. I promised Bob I would if ... if anything ever happened. I know he would do the same for me. Give my love to everyone. I love you Sarah. God Bless you all.

Andy

TO: Robert Hammons, Sr.   FROM: Lt. Andrew
      215 Crescent Drive   McMillan
      Macon, GA   MAC – SOG ...

Dear Mr. Hammons:

It is with deep regret that I fulfill this promise to my friend Bob. Your son was my best friend and respected by all. He believed deeply in what he was doing. Your son truly died a hero. He saved many of us. We were caught in the open and Bobby laid down suppressive fire for over seven minutes. He lay behind a small berm no more than eight inches high. Withering fire was coming from all directions. His actions allowed us to regroup and call for air cover. He not only saved us; he basically saved the whole convoy. Some of the trucks were carrying wounded. Major Drake has recommended Bobby for a Silver Star. His absence leaves a void in the 123rd. Please let Uncle Art and me know if there is anything we can do for your family.

God Bless you all.

Lt. Andrew McMillan

———————————————————

TO: Sarah Ann McMillan   FROM: Lt. Andrew
       Sarah Ann McMillan   McMillan
                                    MAC – SOG ...

Dear Sarah:

I love and miss you Darling. Sorry it's been so long since I've written. Things are heating up a bit. I've been pretty pre-occupied here of late. Recon is getting more difficult. Insurgents seem to be everywhere. I hear there may be an official inquiry into last month's ambush.

Major Drake is raising hell. They keep putting him off. Oh, I got the care package. Thank the ladies at church for all of 1st platoon. The cookies were great. We will be leaving early so I must sign off. Give my love to Mom and Uncle Art. I love you all. God Bless.

Andy

———————————————————

TO: Col. Harold C. Chuckworth
     Commander, MAC – SOG
     Command One, 2nd Battalion,
     Ranger Co, LRRP, Attc.
     24th Mech. Infantry Div.,
     Bagdad, Iraq

FROM: Maj. W. H. Drake
Dep. Com., MAC – SOG
2nd Battalion, Ranger
Co., 123, Attc 24th
Mech. Infantry Div
LRRP Command

Col. Chuckworth:

I was quite surprised at your response Col. I was well within my purview as Dep. Commander to request an inquiry. The 123rd Co. has suffered twenty-seven casualties and ten men from 2nd platoon are still MIA. No less than twenty men under my command are overdue on their rotation, and the 123rd has taken on every Class A assignment for the last ninety days. The continued rumors of an intelligence failure are causing a lapse in morale. My request was on behalf of my men as much as it was the security of 2nd Battalion. I ask you to reconsider Col. Chuckworth.

                                   Maj. W. H. Drake

TO: Maj. W. H. Drake
     Dep., Com., MAC – SOG
     Ranger Co., 123 ...

FROM: Maj. W. H. Drake
Dep. Com., MAC – SOG

Command One ...

Maj. Drake:

Your concern for the security of 2nd Battalion is noted. Your requests are denied. All of them. The 123rd attached Ranger Co. will do its historic duty, without question, to the last man if necessary. I suggest that if you properly disciplined your men they would not give merit to rumors. The ambush of June 9th was unavoidable. We are at war Maj. Drake. I expect you and the 123rd to act accordingly. As soon as this unnecessary inquiry is concluded, I will deal with your insubordination.

Col. Harold C. Chuckworth

TO: Maj. W. H. Drake   FROM: Capt. Frank
      Dep., Com., MAC – SOG Cromwell, MD. PPS
      2nd Battalion ...   2nd Battalion, Med Corp.
                         Attc, 24th Mech.
                         Infantry Div.

Maj. Drake:

It is my considered opinion that after reviewing Lt. Andrew McMillan's last psychological profile he be pulled from active duty immediately. He is suffering from severe Post Traumatic Stress Syndrome as a result of the June 9th ambush of the Baghdad convoy. I have written directly to Col. Chuckworth, to no avail. I feel it my duty to warn you of his condition.

Unfortunately my superiors do not agree with my diagnosis. I will be contacting the A. G. about this matter.

Capt. F. Cromwell, MD, PPS
2nd Battalion, Med Corp ...

TO: Lt. Andrew McMillan   FROM: Author
      MAC – SOG ...   McMillan
                                  P. O. Box 100 ...

Dear Andy:

I know things are tough son, but it's been so long since you have written. We heard about the investigation on the news. Why that bastard Chuckworth is still in command ... Well I know the wheels of military justice grind slowly, but another ambush? Son, you have got to hang on. Believe me, I understand. I was in DaNang when your father was killed. It affected my concentration so bad I almost got myself killed several times. Andy, the pain will pass. Just hang on until it does. It will pass. Everyone here is fine, just worried. Oh yeah, the farm subsidies didn't pass. We will just sell the west block. It was idle anyway. Just hang on son. We all love you. God Bless.

Uncle Art

TO:	Col. Harold C. Chuckworth	FROM: Lt. Col. Ralph
	Commander, MAC – SOG	DeWitt
	Command One ...	FROM: Lt. Col. Ralph
		DeWitt
		Baghdad Iraq, Baghdad
		Sector

Col. Chuckworth:

Harry, we have known each other for a long time. I write this letter as a friend. I hope my next one will not be in my official capacity as J. A. G. of this sector. The old man is on my ass Harry. I just received a file from INCOM and it contained your last three replies to Maj. Drake of the 123rd. I had to polish the general's brass to get him to let me clean this up unofficially. Several people up high are receiving real bad press from the families of the June 9th ambush. The August 22nd incident has been worse. I got to tell you Harry; your last reply to Maj. Drake was considered a direct threat by our office. It's not my call Col., but everyone in C. D. I believes the Al-Haq are reliable. And scuttlebutt has it your sending the 123rd out on a C-A. If the Al-Haq is right again ... Well it will cost you Col. Oh yes, Maj. Drake has let it be known he has already notified Sen. Drake. You're playing a very dangerous game. Harry, please take this under consideration.

Lt. Ralph DeWitt

J. A. G. 24th ...

TO: Lt. Andrew McMillan   FROM: Maj. W. H.
      (OPERATIONAL   Drake
      DIRECTIVE)   Dep., Com.,
      MAC – SOG ...   MAC – SOG
                                   24th ...

Andy, I did what I could. If it means anything I've contacted Dad. I'm afraid it won't help in time for this next one. That fucker Chuckworth has assigned us direct escort on a hot one. Word has it I am to be relieved of command if I survive this. I will be with the 123rd this time. Go ahead and requisition whatever we need. I'll sign it!! It will surely get bad out there. Chuckworth thinks this will get him a star. I'm also trying to get some air cover. The Col. seems to balk at every safety measure available. 0400 Andy, may God go with us Lt.

Maj. Drake
Dep., Com., MAC – SOG ...

_____

TO: Maj. W. H. Drake
      Dep., Com., MAC – SOG
      2nd Battalion, Range Co. 123
      Attc. 24th Infantry Div.

* * * O P. D I R. E Q U I P R E Q * * * (op. Eqp. Invoice)

15 ... M 1026 HMMWV (Humvee)

(4, MB – 50 cal. mountings) 4, MBG .50 cal. mounting

(6, M – 60 mountings)

27 ... SAW 249

(60,000 Rnds. SS – 109 5.56 ammo)

(300, 200 Rnds. assault packs)

117 ... M – 69 Fragmentation grenades

12 ... M – 60, BMG

(2200 Rnds, M – 127, 12.7 NATO Ammo)

(All personal weapons to be charged by individuals)

1 CCCP (Soviet) RPG – 7, 5 inserts (Captured, Supply)

Note: Lt. Mac, I gave you all the M-67 frags we have and all the M60 ammo. Say Mac, I don't know what the hell is going on; no one seems to. But yall keep yalls heads down. All the 24th is praying for the 123rd. don't know what you will do with the RPG's, but Maj. Drake said he'd take full responsibility. I guess you know what Fuckworth has planned for him. Oh yeah, these inserts are the new copper-based magnesium. Supposed to penetrate 300mm of plate. Good luck Andy.

Lt. J. C. Moore
24th Infantry Sup. Mag.

Associated Press Bulletin:

A fierce attack on another Baghdad convoy was beaten back by heavily armed Rangers and helicopter gunships. A battle ensued for over an hour Monday, leaving at least five American soldiers dead and twenty wounded. Over fifty insurgents were killed * * * in a separate incident a highly decorated officer, Colonel Harold C. Chuckworth was killed and his driver critically injured when his vehicle was struck by an RPG. Col. Chuckworth had come under criticism recently for his failure to pay heed to certain intelligence channels considered reliable by many. The Colonels body will be flown back to the States for the funeral. * * *

In Far Northern Iraq ...

_____

TO: Author McMillan   FROM: Lt. Andrew
     P. O. Box ...   McMillan
                             364ᵗʰ Medical Center
                             364ᵗʰ Medical Center

Uncle Art:

I hope I haven't hurt you all too bad by not writing. I couldn't. Uncle Art, you always taught me that sometimes a man's heart is contrary to his thinking. You have been like a Father to me. If Dad had lived I would be telling him this now. I hope you can forgive me.

There was something I felt I had to do ...

The Weaker Vessel

1st Place – Expressions, 2005

Throughout history the female in all cultures, in every age and in all lands has been portrayed as the weaker of the sexes. And while - on average - the female of our species is smaller and perhaps not as physically strong - pound for pound - as the male, does this qualify her as the weaker vessel?

There is no doubt that women have been subjected to a double standard throughout history. That standard which haunted women in times of old is with us still. Even in our most civilized societies, with changes in civil law and intensive efforts to change stereotyping, the double standard yet exists. Many believe that the nature of the learned female role has attributed to our double standard. This has to be true to a degree.

Women, universally repressed and often abused, have been expected to act out the part of the weaker vessel. When she does not, trouble ensues. History is replete with the terrible consequence that results when women do not conform to their expected roles.

The witch hunts in England and early America are prime examples of how ingrained the role model is, and how dangerous violating that model can be. Of course, there were many factors involved in the witch hunt craze. But the fact that more women confessed to being witches freely than confessed under duress is puzzling. As Hugh Trevor-Roper points out in his essay on the subject, for a woman without any real authority in society a belief in such powers could prove quite attractive, despite its hazards. Who is to blame but men for such desperate and bizarre actions of the part of women?

The oppression of women is an undeniable fact of life. Even in our modern time the abject abuse of women is a way of life in much of our world. Women live under unspeakable oppression in many third world countries. Why this is the case one can only speculate. But again the attitudes of men are the root cause. Whether in the name of Chauvin or Muhammad there is something terribly unnatural about the repression or abuse of women. They are our mothers, wives, sisters and daughters. They are our other halves. The radical attitudes of men who would abuse or degrade women represent nothing less than a division in the human race.

It is said that prostitution is the second oldest profession, behind soldiering. (Both institutions created and continued by men.) This is perhaps the first example of the woman asserting her gender traits to even the playing field. And whether men will admit it or not, it is our weakness that makes this possible.

In fact, every exploitation of the woman is a by-product of our vices. Every illicit abuse of women is because of some frailty in us. Yet as with the witch fixation of the 15th and 16th century, women still often bear the pain of our psychosis.

As Phyllis Chester writes in <u>Women and Madness:</u> "No longer are women sacrificed as voluntary or involuntary witches. They are instead; taught to sacrifice themselves for newly named heresies. Today more women are being hospitalized for psychiatric problems than at any time in history." Chester charges this to the nature of the learned female role, the oppression of women and role confusion in our modern age. She further observes, "There is less and less use, and literally no place for them in the only place they 'belong' – within the family. Many newly useless women are emerging more publicly into insanity".

While women have in recent years moved out of the traditional role of mother, our society still bears her signature. Not a human being walks the earth that is not an example of considerable sacrifice a woman made. Just as a woman has a special bond with the child a man can never know, so she has with the entire human race.

It is a sad irony that the most often recorded last words of a dying soldier are cries for his mother.

Conclusion:

As the first man romped in the Garden of Eden he was lonely. What better companion to share the world than woman. We were given stewardship over the earth and all on it. Our weakness is reflected in our resultant behavior. We have treated our women no better than we have treated our earth. This is not to say women can do no wrong - they do - they are, after all, only human. The fact is: woman was given to us as a gift. The most wonderful gift a loving Father could give His male children. It is time she be treated accordingly!!

Sources Used:

Brownmiller, Susan; <u>Against Our Will: Men Women and Rape</u>

Chester, Phyllis; <u>Women and Madness</u>

Masson, Jeffrey; <u>A Dark Science – Women Sexuality and Psychiatry in the Nineteenth Century</u>

Trever-Roper, Hugh; <u>The European Witch Craze of the Sixteenth and Seventeenth Centuries and Other Essays</u>

Sigmund Freud, Psycho - Enigma
(1856 – 1939)

2nd Place – Expressions, 2005

Sigmund Freud's legacy is a bewildering mix of contradictions. He contributed much to our Present-day understanding of psychology. He promoted healthier attitudes towards more humane treatment of children, mental patients and prisoners.

However Freud's ground-breaking work was, unfortunately, tainted by his personal bias and bizarre imagination. It is truly amazing that much of the mythology laid down for us by Sigmund Freud is still accepted as credible in the light of what we now know of the man.

Being a man of his time he subscribed to a good deal of the quackery that had preceded him. Much of his work was so outlandish as to border on the absurd. Just as many professional people who followed Freud, he was prone to believe in the fantastic.

An example of this is how impressed Freud was by the work of Jean-Martin Charcot. In 1885, the young Freud studied under Charcot for a few months. The experience so impressed Freud that he changed his field of study from Neuropathology to Psychopathology. And so, Sigmund Freud, the father of psychoanalysis was born. It is telling that his mentor, Charcot, was judged harshly by his contemporaries. Charcot's theories and treatment were referred to as "Charcot's Circus." And just as his theories fell into disrepute after his death in 1893, so Freud's similar theory of repression is now being questioned.

Until recently, Freud's pronouncements were considered substantially true despite the many oddities surrounding his methodology. Freud's critics point to his extravagant use of cocaine. The new drug - only discovered and synthesized a decade earlier – was proclaimed a miracle by Freud.

In <u>Freudian Fallacy</u>, E. M. Thornton argues that all of Freud's theories were products of cocaine hallucinations. Other followers of Freudian theory contest this assertion. But many of his letters to his friend, Wilhelm Fleiss, are filled with obsessive concern over his nose and its secretions. Freud applied cocaine as a curative. No doubt the cocaine was responsible for his runny nose to begin with.

More serious than his vice of cocaine use was his belief that it could cure almost any ailment. Freud was a major force behind the popular notion that cocaine was a cure for morphine addiction. Even when case after case proved that cocaine use only compounded the morphine addict's problems, he rationalized that a "weak will" was the cause of the cocaine treatment failing. He remained unshaken in his belief even after his close friend Fleischl died in delirium from cocaine toxification.

Other detractors point to Freud's relationship to his patients. It seems that all of Freud's patients were young, attractive, wealthy women. Freud himself writes, "I cannot imagine bringing myself to delve into the psychical mechanism of a hysteria in anyone who struck me as low-minded and repellent." There is no denying that Freud was obsessed with sex. He explicitly blamed hysteria on "precocious experience of sexual relations with actual excitement of the genitals, resulting from sexual abuse." He was convinced that female masturbation caused hysteria.

Freud's theory of personality development focuses on repression and the subconscious. His concepts such as division in the psyche and infantile sexuality force us to consider Mrs. Thornton's allegations that cocaine had indeed colored Freud's thinking.

The most damning aspect of Freud's work is his theory of repression and his obsession with incest. The mythology that developed from Freud's theory of repressed memories contributed directly to the False Memory Syndrome craze of the 20th century.

Conclusion ...

When Sigmund Freud's work, theories, methodology and ethics are taken fully into consideration, its hard not to wince. It seems the history of psychiatry is not without a sense of irony.

Sigmund Freud, a man obsessed with sex who used and freely distributed a dangerous drug, a man who refused to accept responsibility for killing several people, including a close friend, a man who's ethical conduct would land him in prison today, this is our father of psychoanalysis.

Sources Used ...

Freud, Sigmund, Standard Edition of the Complete Psychological Works of Sigmund Freud

Greenbaum, Adolf, Foundations of Psychoanalysis

Haberman, Vicktor J., A Criticism of Psychoanalysis (Journal of Abnormal Psychology)

Pendergrast, Mark, Victims of Memory

Thornton, E. M., Freudian Fallacy

Woods, Garth, Myth of Neurosis

Yates, Frances, The Art of Memory

How Crucifixion Kills

3rd Place – Expressions, 2005

The crucifixion and resurrection of Jesus of Nazareth is the founding event of Christianity. Through the centuries theories have flourished that attempt to explain the resurrection as having natural causes. If one accepts the historically well - documented events surrounding the crucifixion and claimed resurrection of Jesus, these various theories can bring questions to mind because miracles are inherently difficult to believe in.

However difficult the resurrection is to believe, naturalistic explanations of Jesus surviving his ordeal on the cross are just as difficult to accept. When analyzed from a medical perspective the difficulty in accepting one of the many survival theories increase.

One such theory postulates that Jesus had been drugged (the sponge dipped in vinegar, Mark 15:36). That he appeared dead and was then taken to safety by His disciples. At the turn of the century Karl Venturini suggested that when Jesus passed out he was taken from the cross pre-maturely and later revived in the tomb. These are but a few of the many explanations for the resurrection of Jesus.

For many people who wonder about this conflict of ideas, a legitimate question stands out: "Is it physically possible to survive what Jesus suffered?"

The fact is most people don't even know what kills a victim of crucifixion. If one researches this perplexing subject the details are grizzly. How does the cross kill? To answer this question medical science can help. In answering this question one must start with the Roman Flogging.

The Flogging:

The Roman flogging was a brutal affair, done with whip like implement known as the flagellum. It had several braided strands of heavy leather. These strands had pieces of copper or lead interwoven into it. The standard flogging was forty lashes, save one. Custom required error to the side of mercy. This seems a rather moot point because long before the flogging was finished the victims back, ribcage, legs and buttocks were reduced to tatters of bloody flesh. In fact, it was not uncommon for the subject to die before the sentence was carried out. History tells us that Jesus did survive the flogging. Having lost a great deal of blood the victim would suffer hypovolemic shock, including a loss of blood pressure and loss of kidney function. It was in this condition that Jesus collapsed while carrying the cross.

The Crucifixion:

The victim is laid down on the crossbeam (patibulum) and metal spikes are driven through the wrist about an inch below the palms. This would put the spike through the median nerve – the largest nerve in the arm. To grasp the intensity of the pain this causes, one only need consider the word <u>excruciating</u> which means, "out of the cross." The feet are nailed in a similar fashion.

Cause of Death:

As the victim hangs on the cross both shoulders become dislocated. Being fixed in the inhale position, one must push up to exhale and relieve the pressure on the diaphragm. As the victim struggles to breathe, the tarsal bone in the foot soon grinds against the spike in the feet. The breathing would slow down causing carbon dioxide to dissolve as carbonic acid producing an increase in acidity in the blood. This increase in acidity leads to an irregular heart beat as well as pericardial and pleural effusion – a buildup of fluid around the heart and lungs. It is a striking coincidence that John describes "water and blood" as coming from the wound inflected by the Roman soldiers spear thrust, (John 19:34). The pericardial and pleural effusion would have appeared as a clear liquid. It is at this point one must ask, "How much can the human body stand?" As the ordeal continues the victim finally succumbs to asphyxia - induced cardiac arrest.

Conclusion:

If one carefully considers the historical evidence for the trial, crucifixion and resurrection of Jesus and believes he lived after, only two possibilities exist. One, he survived a severe flogging. Then he survived enough injury to kill several people. Then he survived certain asphyxiation and cardiac arrest. Then he survived a spear thrust that penetrated his heart and lung. Then he was later able to walk away. Seems unlikely.

The other possibility is that He was resurrected by supernatural forces, just as He predicted He would be.

Sources Used:

James B. Conant, Science and Common Sense

William D. Edwards., et al. "On the Physical Death of Jesus Christ". Journal of the American Medical Association (March 21, 1986), 1455-63.

Dale Forman, Crucify Him

Martin Hengel, Crucifixion in the Ancient World

Harold Mattingly, Roman Imperial Civilization

Josh McDowell, Evidence That Demands an Answer

Peter W. Stoner and Robert C. Newman, Science Speaks

Lee Stroble, The Case for Christ

Ode to Osama

Expressions, 2005

Osama has a funny belief
He lives on hatred and grief
Cursing all who he hates
And resigned to his fate
And death will be his only relief

Osama hates the red, white and blue
And his followers blind to what is true
From the mountains up high
He sent others to die
Then ran like all cowards do

Osama did what good terrorists do
Died hating the Christian and Jew
Expecting his virgins with glee
He asked an angel when Allah might be
Saint Peter scornfully replied ... "Allah who ..."

Trapped

Expressions, 2005

I cry out from the depth of my sorrow,
Within these walls that are my home

The cries echo back from the cold hard
Walls I have constructed

The walls I have constructed over the
Course of my wretched life

Walls built from the bricks of wild ambitions
And reckless conduct

Bonded with the crumbling mortar of limitless
Self-confidence and false beliefs

The walls that now cover me in shadows and
Block me from the light of day

Walls that threaten to collapse around me
Crushing me with the weight of my despair

The rubble of these walls, like memories I
Cannot escape

Only through the collapse of these walls is
There a chance of escaping them

So, if the collapse of these walls means either
Death or freedom, let them fall

For as long as they stand, I remain a prisoner
Forever trapped.

This Bond we Share

Expressions, 2005
(2007 – 1st Place w/Shot Caller Press)

This bond we share is sealed with blood
And binds us with its weight
We bear the scars of meeting
Dealt by the hand of fate

As chance would have us enemies
In a contest … kill or be killed
The stage now set, the die was cast
In a moment our fates were sealed

Our lives both changed forever
In the twinkling of an eye
We met as strangers, face to face
In a match where one must die

We both had ground we had to stand
And neither one could yield
So the ground that lay between us
Became our battlefield

Only we can know the truth
About the guilt that we both bear
This truth that we cannot escape
Like this bitter bond we share

William Davis

This bond we share, as old as time
Born of tears and pain
Sealed forever in our hearts
And words cannot explain

How in the heat of battle
Two warriors join as one
You had only duty
And I ... no place to run

Each believing that we were right
We struck out, yet both were spared
Now we must live with what we did
And this bond, forever shared.

Dedicated to Officer Langford ...

Chapter 6

Students

Honorable Mention – Expressions, 2004
(1st Annual Publishers Award)

It was an officer Vasha had in his sight picture, though he couldn't be sure of his rank. His breathing slowed. He was aware of his new spotter, Anton, reaffirming the range ... approximately two hundred meters.

This would be Vasha's thirty-fifth kill, though he knew he had only wounded the last eight or nine. His comrade blamed the American rifle he used, but Vasha knew better. He knew the Springfield, chambered for 30-06, was every bit as accurate as the Russian Mosin-Nagant in 7.62 x 57.

His instructor, the famous Russian expert sniper, Master Sergeant Vasily Zaitsev knew this as well. Zaitsev had over two hundred and fifty kills now and was a Soviet hero.

Zaitsev had handpicked Vasha for special training in the Cauldron. The Cauldron, as it was called by Russians and Germans alike, was a perfect hell. The broken, burning ruins of Stalingrad had once been home to nearly a million people. Now, after four months of fighting, only demons and mad-men resided there. Like a giant disembodied spirit, a choking cloud of dust and burn cordite hung continuously in the air. The stench of death was everywhere. Day by day, men killed without thought until they died in the hands of an enemy, succumbed to frostbite or starved to death.

As Vasha took another breath, he let the crosshairs drift a little. His finger increased the pressure slightly on the trigger.

For a moment he thought he would lose the shot. But the officer just stood still. *Didn't he know better?* Vasha knew that Zaitsev was expecting a clean kill. The seconds passed ... he squeezed the trigger and felt the American rifle buck in his arms. Regaining the sight picture quickly, he waited for the bullet to strike. A distinct puff of dust exploded from the officer's hip.

He heard Anton's cold and professional voice announce, "Low, to the left ..."

Vasha was afraid of this. This new spotter was good and gave exact reports.

"Vasha, Come with me." Zaitsev spoke with sharpness. They crawled to a nearby wall and stood. Already German machine gun fire was being sprayed in their direction.

"Why, Vasha? And don't give me that rubbish about a wounded soldier being more trouble than a dead one. Have you lost your nerve for killing?"

Vasha did believe the military doctrine of wounding being more costly to the enemy than killing. But that was not what started him wounding German soldiers. In the midst of this brutality, his early Christian teachings had returned to him – the belief that all life is sacred. It had come to him as he sighted in on a young German Corporal a couple of months ago. All of a sudden he saw himself in the crosshairs. He realized this young blond infantryman had no more understanding of the catastrophe that had befallen the world then he. For some reason he let the crosshairs drift. The young German who had exposed himself so foolishly had been spared. Saved by a flak jacket and the drifting aim of Vasha.

"I know that is not the reason for you missing such an easy kill. Tell me, Vasha, how can you respect the lives of these gray-green slugs that have so devastated our country?"

Vasha remained silent.

"Do you know what it would cost you were it known you spared a German officer? Execution or a punishment battalion. Do you want that, Vasha? Do you think a German sniper will only wound you?"

Vasha leaned the Springfield rifle against the wall and spoke. "I can only answer for myself, Sergeant."

Zaitsev touched Vasha's shoulder and spoke softly. "Perhaps God will spare you in your weakness Vasha, but I doubt it, not here. Know that in showing mercy, you risk your life in more ways than one."

Zaitsev turned and walked away leaving Vasha alone with his thoughts.

*****

Out in front of the German lines, young Corporal Schmitt handled the bullet Doctor Kroner had removed from his body two months ago. The bullet had penetrated the flak jacket and lodged between two ribs. Doctor Kroner had expressed surprise at the corporal's survival. Schmitt was one of the few to survive the sniper who used the American rifle. Others had expressed surprise as well. Among them, the famous German sniper, SS Colonel Heinz Thornwald. Colonel Thornwald had been assigned the task of eliminating the Soviet hero, Zaitsev.

It was Colonel Thornwald's visit to the aid station that young Corporal Schmitt's proficiency with the Mauser rifle had been called to his attention. That was two months ago. Schmitt was now the Colonel's top student. He was hoping for his twenty-first kill. He carried the American 30-06 slug as a good luck charm.

The no-man's land between the ever-shifting front lines was a perfect hunting ground for snipers. Square mile after square mile of rubble. Burnt out buildings by the hundreds.

Artillery spotters, radio wire men, forward observers ... all targets. Any lost soul, a target.

The psychological damage the sniper does is even more important than his kills. Corporal Schmitt understood this and wondered about the recent string of wounding his squad had suffered. Eight ... or was it nine now in the last month or so. All were shot by the sniper using the American rifle. This fellow had made well over twenty clean kills from as far away as four hundred meters. Why was he now missing? Or was he? Schmitt knew the report on his own injury – the shot had been from less than one hundred and fifty meters. No, the Russian had not missed. But why would he spare a German soldier?

Colonel Thornwald had commented that the sniper using the American rifle was just demonstrating the barbaric Russian mentality. Enjoying the suffering he inflicted. But every victim the Russian had not killed was back in Germany convalescing. Except for Schmitt who had volunteered for Thornwald's sniper team.

No, this Russian was wounding deliberately. The rounds were too well placed. Schmitt, as all German soldiers, knew of the Russian punishment battalions. Men used to clear mine fields and to draw enemy fire. Humans who are totally expendable. Why would a Russian soldier risk this? The question had plagued Schmitt until it was affecting his concentration.

"Achtung," the low voice of Schmitt's spotter called his attention to shadows at the base of a pile of rubble about two hundred meters away. As Schmitt rested his sight picture on the rubble, a light flashed in the shadows. Moments later he heard an impact and a cry of pain.

An officer crumpled to the ground, shot through the hip. In the ensuing confusion of administering aid, Schmitt is made aware of the officer's "luck" to have only been wounded. He knew this was not luck, but a well-placed shot. Why? Why would he spare a German officer?

As Schmitt surveyed the area, his sight picture focused on a piece of broken wall. Two Russian soldiers stood. Then one walked away. The lone soldier reached for his rifle leaning against the wall.

Then Schmitt noticed, the rifle was not a Russian Mosin-Nagant but a Springfield – the sniper who used the American rifle.

Schmitt quickly drew a bead. The crosshairs of the telescopic sight rested on the center mass of the target. An easy shot and his twenty-first kill.

But as Schmitt drew his three-quarter lung-full of air and began to squeeze the trigger, his crosshairs dropped slightly and began to drift. The Mauser roared and jarred Schmitt's body.

When he regained his sight picture, he saw nothing. Corporal Schmitt's spotter reported, "Low and to the left. It's a hit but I can't confirm a kill. Better luck next time, eh Schmitt?"

Sandstorm

Chapter 1 ... The Copper Scrolls

Expressions, 2004

Was it a second-century AD treasury related to the Bar Kokhbo Revolt against Roam? Perhaps the treasure belonged to the temple in Jerusalem – or to the Essenes.

To whom the treasure may have belonged was rendered academic now that a possible location had been agreed upon. The Copper Scrolls found in the caves around the Dead Sea in 1952 were now, for the most part, deciphered. They believed the location of the treasures described in the scrolls were clear.

The only thing clear to Davige was that the arguing was over and the search would begin. As security adviser for the team he had tried to warn these scholars that the fragile peace between Israel and New Palestine would not last forever. Not to mention that what they were doing was technically illegal, and they would be less than one kilometer from the new border. He also knew that the leader of the expedition – the internationally famous Ulrich Vanderburk – would stop at nothing to prove his theory correct.

Ulrich Vanderburk was a man of exceptional credentials, drive and nearly unlimited political connections. He had to be to cajole the president of Israel, the Prime Minister of New Palestine, the Governor of Judea and several segments of the international community to support his expedition – an expedition destined to cause a conflict that could possibly lead to a third world war. This was the expedition William Davige was to provide security for.

Davige listened as Professor Ezra Ben-Dothan explained to Akbar Hahmed – the head of the newly formed Arab

Confederacy – why it was worth the effort and risk. Davige had heard it all before. Still, hearing Ben-Dothan talk on this subject was mesmerizing. His wire frame glasses jiggling as he spoke, his long white hair bouncing as he stood, no longer able to sit as he explained. At the end of a long litany of past Israeli treasures he concluded with ... "Clearly gentlemen, over one hundred and fifty tons of gold and precious gems lie in the Kindron Valley in the wilderness of Judea. Even more important, the history of mankind. Information that could transform our very world. Any risk is worth the find."

Ben-Dothan's words hung in the air. The professor, the world's leading Qumranologist was not above using greed to appeal to whoever necessary to make the discovery he believed accompany the treasure they may find. And it was working – one could almost see dollar signs in Hahmed's eyes. He rubbed his pock-marked face with his hands. All eyes were on this big Arab. As the Arab Confederacy representative, he was effectively the last obstacle to the expedition. After many moments of silence the big Arab leaned back in his seat. Looking across the table he addressed the expedition's leader.

"Now Mis-ter Van-de-burk, do you believe the good professor's calculations are correct? Both on the estimates of the find and the location?" Vanderburk stood holding a folder. A tall imposing figure of a man, he held the folder out.

"You've seen ... we all have seen the data. While no orthographic system matches the ones used in the copper scrolls, they are authentic. No doubt. The fact that it has no parallel to any other scrolls found in the Qumran Caves speaks for its authenticity, not against it. I believe professor Ben-Dothan's calculations, and mine, are completely correct."

Speaking as he always did – as if his words could not be questioned – Vanderburk eased back into his seat. Hahmed looked almost shaken. Did he believe all he was hearing? He stood and leaned over the table.

"Gentlemen, let us cut to the heart of this matter. We all know this expedition stands on somewhat ... questionable legal grounds. Questionable indeed. Only by the hope of gain by many has this planning come this far. We all know that a portion of ancient Hyrcania lies well within New Palestine. Should any ... incident cause conflict we all know the possible consequence."

At this Hahmed waved his hand at Davige gesturing for him to speak. Davige stood and cleared his throat as he stepped to a large map.

"Ehem ... well gentlemen this all hinges on the accuracy of the surveyors. I believe they are at least very close. The area in question lies behind what is known locally as the Five Hills of Hasmon. Now according to international agreement we should be able to work, completely legally in area 5-b. If the team's calculations and the satellite infrared imaging are on the money, the underground staircase mentioned in the copper scrolls should be accessible ... from underground. As we all in this room know, this will be the first expedition of this kind in the history of archeology. We will all be disguised as a border surveying team. We will have a minimum of equipment. Of course we have all accepted the risk involved should we be actually caught trespassing into New Palestine ..." Glances were exchanged as Davige's words brought home the reality of just how risky this expedition was.

"Needless to say, being caught, under any circumstances, infringing on New Palestine's territory, we would be subject to summary execution."

Then a tall rail of a man, with a face like a human rat interjected forcefully,

"Yes gentlemen, but I give you my word as the New Palestinian's representative of this expedition, the New Palestinian authorities who count, know of this expedition and will turn a blind eye to certain details to assure gain." Then Davige countered with a question.

"And Mr. Hak-Nah, suppose the Hezmon know of this? Or the Kevesh for that matter?" Davige turned from the map to fully address the group.

"Gentlemen, trespassing into New Palestine, as hazardous as that may be the least of our worries. Should the Palestinian Hezmon or the Israeli Kevesh, either one get wind of such cooperation between Israel and New Palestine, there will be hell to pay. That's not to mention the bitterness of the several thousand border soldiers who stare down the sights of their machine guns at each other day after day. We could be shot by accident. A single mortar round could put us in the middle of a major military engagement ...

"Area 5-b is surrounded by the lesser plain of Ein Getti. While we will have good cover for our work, only two hundred meters in any direction and our cover evaporates. We have no escape route should hostilities break out." At this a hand was raised. A short balding man timidly sought permission to speak. Davige noticed and offered the floor.

"Mr. Zadok, did you have something?" The man stood slowly looking around yet avoiding eye contact.

"My question is in regards to the passage professor Ben-Dothan had earlier mentioned. The one about God's protection of the treasure against the impure of heart." At this Hak-Nah laughed out loud.

"Ha, who better to be concerned with God's judgment than the descendants of the deposed temple priest? That is what we need, a bit of humor in an otherwise somber discussion." Hahmed held his arms up and spoke, focusing sternly at Hak-Nah.

"Despite our earlier agreement to leave religion out of this, I will allow this question on the table, if for no other reason because Mr. Zadok's concern is legitimate." Hak-Nah's resentment was clear as he spoke.

"Of course the historical significance of your name is not lost Mr. Zadok." At this Vanderburk stood quickly, his chair rattling as he did.

"Gentlemen, this is hardly the time for such a discussion. Mr. Davige has outlined what a dangerous situation we could find ourselves in. I suggest that all conflicting feelings be dispensed with here and now for the sake of success." At this professor Ben-Dothan stood.

"The passage in question is one not yet fully understood. While Mr. Zadok's concerns are certainly legitimate, surely his very presence indicates the purity of our motives. We do know the passage refers to looting. I can advise in all good conscience that on the grounds of our purpose, we are free from any warning in this, as of yet misunderstood passage ..."

The professor's calm demeanor seemed to effect all in the room as he spoke. Before the echo of his words could fade, the American Hum Vees roared to life. Six passengers dressed as Israeli military surveyors were headed into the Judean wilderness. Each one in search of something different.

Is Man Free?

Honorable Mention – Expressions, 2004

Does Man really have freedom of thought? Freedom of Choice? Freedom of action?

The question of man's freedom is a deep one indeed. Freedom can mean many things to many different people. The perception of freedom, mental or physical, is, of course, one of the most perplexing and varying of all human lines of thought.

In today's world, there are so many people living under such different extremes, with such contrasting beliefs that even asking the question boggles one's mind.

Who is the most free? A despot dictator, who through absolute power controls every aspect of social, economic and military life, yet can trust no one? Who, despite his total control, must at all times be on guard against assassination ...?

Or the political prisoner he had imprisoned for speaking out against him in defiant disregard?

Who is most free? The paraplegic confined to a wheelchair, unable to work or move freely and cannot participate in regular social activities ... Or the able bodied man that is illiterate and unemployed, imprisoned by his ignorance.

Who is the freer? The one with physical freedom, but is mentally imprisoned because of emotional difficulties or someone with a clear mind, but limited physical freedom?

The very concept of freedom in human existence is paradoxical. The inevitable conclusion is that the more freedom of thought one has, the more one realizes the limitations that the world places on everyone. Still, despite all the limitations placed on mankind from moral laws, physics, society and his own physical and mental frailties, I personally believe that anyone, to a large degree, is as free as he makes himself. No matter what your lot in life, anyone is free to think, to philosophize, free to speak the truth.

I also believe that freedom must be exercised. Whatever freedom is, to anyone, it must be exercised. Complacency is one of freedom's worst enemies – the enemy of mental as well as physical freedom. There is no absolute freedom, but complacency threatens all concepts of freedom everywhere.

History is replete with examples of men and women who were intellectually free. Winston Churchill, Albert Camus, Martin Luther King, Jr., Joan of Arc, Clara Barton, Esther, and Bob Hope. These people were free thinkers who used their freedom in a very real way to inspire millions of their countrymen at a time when inspiration was badly needed. They used their physical and intellectual freedom to fight for freedom for all.

Despite the great dangers involved, they exercised their freedom. They refused to let their freedom be restricted because of the possible danger involved. They refused to become prisoners of fear. In doing so, they gained a form of freedom not commonly known. They made their freedom by their actions in support of free thought.

Freedom is attainable for those who are willing to search for it, for those not afraid to exercise what freedom they have, and to take risks ...

For those who have struggled to attain it, freedom has meaning that others may never know. Perhaps that is real freedom, freedom that one has to struggle to attain.

A Search for Truth

Honorable Mention – Expressions, 2004

By definition, science is a search for truth. As with any reasonable, sincere search, one should follow the facts no matter where they may lead. This has not always been the case with science, yet the truth has a way of surfacing when least expected. Discoveries by people who refuse to give in to their personal theories or the theories of others continue to act as a corrective and keeps science from stagnating. Just as the theory of a flat earth was dispelled by new facts being brought to light, so other theories have fallen by the wayside.

Spontaneous Generation, the five perfect solids and attempts to turn lead into gold, are examples of ideas that seem ridicules today. Yet, in earlier times these theories represented the science of the day, theories not to be questioned.

A ruling theory that has been accepted as fact for over one hundred years that seems likely to crumble soon is that of Darwinism and Macro-evolution. Built on a good many assumptions, Darwin's theory is now being seriously reconsidered by a new breed of scientist from a wide range of fields who base their ideas on recent findings. Two fields of study have made Darwin's theory of evolution harder and harder for the inquiring mind to accept. Paleontology and microbiology are leading man away from the traditional concepts of life's origins on this planet. In 1909 the Burgess Shale discovery in the Canadian Rockies yielded what is referred to by paleontologists as the Cambrian Explosion.

Richard Dawkins, a leading Darwinist himself, says of the Burgess Shale fossil record, "It is as though they were just planted there, without any evolutionary history." Then came an even more significant find. The Chengjiang discovery in China offers even more varied life forms, all suddenly appearing within the Cambrian Explosion. Even in Darwin's day, the absence of fossil finds representing transitional stages posed an embarrassing enigma for the theory of evolution. Darwinists have long depended on, and anxiously awaited, fossil records to vindicate their theory. Exactly the opposite has happened. This now offers up a major stumbling block for the theory. Microbiology has presented even more compelling questions for the Darwinists.

In only the last few years, discoveries have been made that could not have been fathomed a decade ago, much less in Darwin's day. Very recent discoveries reveal that even single cells are far more complex than previously imagined. Parts and functions of single cells have been discovered that are still unexplained. Microbiologist, Michael Behe of Pennsylvania's Lehigh University has developed a theory of Irreducible Complexity. This theory was developed as he made breakthroughs in cell research. According to this theory, an irreducible complex system cannot function without all of its constituent parts. The system does not acquire function until all parts are in place.

The significance of this is brought into sharp focus by the fact absolutely no one-not one scientist-has published any detailed explanation of the possible evolution of any complex biological system. Any science that claims to have explained something when, in fact they have not, should be called into account. The universal absence of opinion on this subject would not be accepted in any other field of science and it should not be accepted in explaining the origins of life.

While Darwin could not have known of the complexity of the single cell in his day, he did acknowledge the problem of the fossil record. Darwin, to his credit, has left us a method to test his theory. In Darwin's book, The Origin of Species, he states, "If it could be demonstrated that any complex organ existed which could not possibly have been formed by numerous, successive, slight modifications, my theory would absolutely break down."

As Mr. Behe's research has shown, a single cell could comprise several, if not dozens, of irreducibly complex systems. It is therefore difficult to imagine how they may have been formed by numerous, successive, slight modifications.

Even if Darwin's theory is disproved and we are left with no theory at all to replace it, we are better off than to continue in error. At the least we will be free to pursue new ideas ... which of course, is what a search for truth is all about.

Sources Used:

Behe, Michael, Darwin's Black Box

Darwin, Charles, The Origin of Species

Dembski, William, <u>The Design Inference</u>

Denton, Michael, M.D., <u>Evolution: A Theory in Crisis</u>

Gills, James P., M.D., Woodward, Tom, Ph.D., <u>Darwinism under the Microscope: Scientific Evidence Points to Divine Design</u>

Johnson, Philip, <u>Darwinism on Trial</u>

Taxton, Charles, <u>The Mystery of Life's Origin</u>

The Attic

Honorable Mention – Expressions, 2004

I don't go in the attic much
It is a cluttered place, you see;
Full of thoughts, of long-lost things,
And of wants that cannot be.

Somewhere in the attic's reaches,
Exactly where, I do not know,
Lying deep beneath the cobwebs
Are things I stowed there long ago.

Memories of things I've lost
And of others I wish to lose,
Still lying there beneath the dust
Abandoned dreams and unpaid dues.

Still stored among the clutter
The "I love you's" left unsaid;
Stored for keeps, the bitter pain
Of this wayward life I've led.

Feelings stashed there through my life
Hidden ... but never concealed ...
Stacked one on top another,
In this attic, long since filled.

Stored there are all the things in life
That I wish to leave behind,
But still there mingled with the dust,
In this attic ... that is my mind.

Flashing Eyes

Expressions, 2004

A torch of fire in my soul,
And the burning never dies;
Fired by your womanhood,
When you flashed me with your eyes.

My want for you now blazes,
Though I try with all my might;
I am lost, with no control,
Since I have fallen to your sight.

This heart of mine you own,
So easily possessed ...
I saw you look inside me,
I felt my soul caressed.

Our bodies locked together,
As I look deep into your eyes;
The love we make, pours out as one,
And I hear your desperate cries.

I feel your nails now piercing,
And you tightly squint your eyes;
I feel your body's rapture,
And we will not be denied ...

This love you caused to happen,
My heart, an easy prize;
Won by you, with a single glance,
With the flashing of your eyes.

To the most beautiful creature on earth ...
    Mrs. Mary T. Davis.

The Weeping Willow

Expressions, 2004

I took a break from cutting wood
Beneath a willow tree
I drifted off and as I slept,
The willow spoke to me

The willow told me not to fear
As I lay there fast asleep,
All he wanted was to talk
So I asked, "Why do you weep?"

And then the willow spoke again
And much to my surprise,
He told me if I really cared
He would tell me why he cries

"I weep for all the fallen trees
And man's endless quest for wood,
For all the barren wasteland
Where once mighty forest stood"

"I weep for trees of every kind,
For none are safe in any land
Where thoughtless men who do not care
Have saw and ax in hand"

"I weep for birds that have no nest

Because their homes are gone,
Sacrificed for progress
That continues on and on"

"I cry for all the plant life
From mighty oak to tiny fern,
For all the land that's being raped
By men who slash and burn"

And so my eyes were opened
By a willow tree that day
Only one thing I could do,
Put down my ax and go my way

Now I am here to tell the world
What I learned there in my sleep,
That only God can make a tree ...
But men can make them weep.

Dedicated to ... our earth.

141

Chapter 7

Closing Arguments in the Trial of Mr. Gunn

1st Place – Expressions, 2003

(1999 – Honorable Mention w/Pen American)

Bailiff Jester: In the District Court of Blah-blah-blah, any county, any state, U.S.A., Cause Number yak, yak, yak, the State versus Mr. Gunn. Court is now in order, the honorable Judge Gavelbanger presiding. Representing the State, District Attorney, Janet Brady, and Council for the defense, Jefferson Handcock.

The Judge enters the courtroom.

Bailiff Jester: All rise.

Judge Gavelbanger: You all may be seated. I hope today's closing arguments can proceed without the unrestrained emotionalism that has so marked this trial thus far.

The opposing lawyers glared at one another intently, as the jurors sat nervously in their seats. Mr. Gunn sat quietly, leaning to one side awkwardly in his chair at the polished oak defense table. It was obvious that Mr. Gunn couldn't care less about the closing arguments.

Judge Gavelbanger: Are the councilors ready to proceed?

Council for the defense Handcock rises from his seat and addresses Judge Gavelbanger.

Councilor Handcock: Your honor, is it really necessary that my client be cuffed? It's not likely he is going anywhere.

Judge Gavelbanger: The defendant will remain restrained Mr. Handcock, now if you are ready, these proceedings have gone on far too long already.

Councilor Handcock eased from behind the defense table and approached the jurors, who sat waiting for him to speak.

Councilor Handcock: Good morning ladies and gentlemen of the jury, you have a decision to make today. A decision that will have effects that reach far beyond the doors of this courtroom. You have all heard the facts of this case. On the night of some month, certain day, any year, Mr. Gunn and Mr. Addict entered Buddy's Drink up Liquor and robbed and shot to death Mr. Buddy Victim. You have heard eyewitness testimony firmly established that it was Mr. Addict that pulled trigger. Now despite this eyewitness testimony there has arisen a controversy over who actually bears responsibility for the killing. You have heard Mr. Addict claim that it was some sort of an accident. You have heard the eloquent Mrs. Brady argue that Mr. Gunn did the killing. That Mr. Gunn is a heartless, no-feeling, cold-blooded killer. The fact is that Mr. Gunn did enter the Drink up Liquor store with Mr. Addict, and was involved in the shooting of Buddy Victim. But where does the blame rest? ... Who made the conscious decision to pull the trigger? ... You heard Mr. Addict's defense that he was a product of his environment, the victim of a troubled life on drugs, a life of repeated arrests because of his drug use. If Mr. Addict is a product of our society, then how much more is Mr. Gunn, who has used no drugs? ... Ladies and gentlemen, look at Mr. Gunn and tell me if you can say you believe, really honestly believe that he made the decision to shoot down Buddy Victim.

The jury looked long at Mr. Gunn still sitting motionless in his chair.

Defense Councilor Handcock continues: I think not ... Perhaps Mr. Addict and Mr. Gunn are both what we, as a society, have made them ... But that is not the question we seek to answer. You have heard Mrs. Brady damn Mr. Gunn's "kind", and demand his "kind" be banished from our society. But I ask you ladies and gentlemen, how many times in the past has Mr. Gunn's "kind" defended our freedom? ... Does not Mr. Gunn's "kind" defend our rights every day? ... Has Mr. Addict's "kind" made such a contribution in the past? ... I ask that you find Mr. Gunn, not guilty of the death of Buddy Victim.

Councilor Handcock returned to the defense table as the jurors sat pondering his words.

Judge Gavelbanger: Mrs. Brady, are you ready for you closing argument? ...

District Attorney Brady: Yes you're Honor.

District Attorney Brady rose from her chair and stood to face the jurors. She stood quietly for some time before she suddenly turned, pointed directly at Mr. Gunn, her words echoing throughout the courtroom.

District Attorney Brady: Gunn is a killer! You all know it was his bullet that smashed through the forehead of Buddy Victim, splattering his brains in all directions, leaving his wife a widow and his children fatherless.

At the defense table Mr. Gunn showed no reaction to Mrs. Brady's outburst.

District Attorney Brady continues: Yes, Gunn is a killer and he is not even sorry. He has not shown the slightest remorse. His "kind" kill every day, our people, our children and ... he would kill you if he got the chance. If his "kind" are not banished from our society, he will kill us all. "We the people" of this great country have the right to be protected from the "Gunn's" of this world. Is it really important who pulled the trigger? The truth of the matter is, had Mr. Gunn not been there, Buddy Victim might still be alive. It was Mr. Gunn's almost satanic effect on Mr. Addict that caused this shameful killing. It is for that reason that you must find Mr. Gunn guilty of the murder of Buddy Victim. Thank You.

Mrs. Brady walked back to her seat as the jury sat in silence.

Judge Gavelbanger: Ladies and gentlemen of the jury, it is now in your hands. I hope you are able to sort fact from fiction, and set aside all the emotion this case has given rise to and make a decision based on logic. Good luck in your deliberations. The defendant will be returned to the usual confinement until a verdict is rendered. This court stands in recess. Bailiff Jester, if you please ...

Bailiff Jester moved in cautiously towards Mr. Gunn who was still sitting quietly at the defense table.

Bailiff Jester: Come on Mr. Gunn, time to go.

Bailiff Jester yanked at the handcuff's chain. Mr. Gunn shifted from the awkward position he had maintained throughout the trial and slipped lifelessly from the chair, his front sight, and flash suppresser of his sleek barrel striking sharply on the polished surface of the defense table, leaving a distinct dent in the otherwise smooth surface.

Bailiff Jester: Easy on the furniture Gunn, you clumsy bastard!

   Mr. Gunn made no reply as he was escorted out of the courtroom, his high-test polymer buttstock dragging on the floor.

Partial Report on Mannraptor

Expressions, 2003

... with the death of an Estakabrah agent in Ankara Turkey. Other Estakabrah agents were close behind the subject and followed him to Bucharest, Romania. One of the agents, Emil Yerevan was later found dead. The cause of death was the same as in all the rest; crushed cervical vertebra, ruptured diaphragm and a fractured skull. Yerevan made the sixth victim killed in this fashion. His partner, Ismir Sirakaya has so far done what no one else has managed to do, talk to Mannraptor face to face and walk away. Sirakaya is now being held in a maximum security facility for his protection. His description confirms others: white male, 5'10" tall, approximately one hundred sixty to seventy pounds, blond hair, and blue eyes. Sirakaya had only been out of visual contact with Yerevan for about ten minutes. He is certain he saw the subject leaving the alley where Yerevan's body was found. Yet Mannraptor showed no signs of having killed a man in a violent struggle. By all accounts Emil Yerevan was a formidable adversary, an ex-Spetsnaz (Soviet Special Forces) and a former instructor of hand-to-hand combat for the organization.

Less than seventy-two hours later one of our agents in Sao Paulo, Brazil was informed by a local operative that a man answering to the subject's description signed the registry at the Santo Andre Hotel as Boris Mannraptor. The agent, Carl Hobbs, reported this to his superior, Salvador Rios. Rios ordered all available personnel to converge on the Santo Andre Hotel. The special operations unit of the Sao Paulo police was also mobilized. The hotel was completely surrounded within the hour. The hotel and grounds area were searched for over twelve hours. No sign of the subject. This isn't the first time Mannraptor has managed to evade an intense dragnet of experienced agents supported by local authorities.

Two days later Carl Hobbs's and Salvador Rio's mutilated bodies were found floating in the Paraiba do Sul.

- Known Origins of Boris Mannraptor –

Two competing theories exist. Theory One: He was born Boris Puskin in Moscow. There is no date of birth available, but he allegedly attended a University in Kazan in 1990. Theory Two: He was born Boris Mann in Munich, Germany in 1962. He was a physics major at a technical school there and went to work at the Chernobyl Nuclear plant just before the accident. A report released by the Soviet Minister of Foreign Information lists a "Boris Mann" as having died in a re-vent shaft of the number 4 reactor. The report continues, but becomes as fanciful as to be of no practical benefit. It has him surfacing again in Kazan in 1996 where by coincidence we see the first victim with wounds similar to those we are now encountering. A blond haired, blue eyed man of striking resemblance to the Boris Mannraptor in our investigation appears in a photo taken on a Cheboksary – Volga river trolley in 1996. It is obvious the Soviet authorities are taking these reports more seriously than our director is. His last reply will be attached herein.

* * * Report from Interpol * * *

Magdenburg Germany: A report filed by Deutschland Polazi Captain Rudolf Breman should be put before our Director as soon as possible. It contains a DNA analysis of blood recovered from the scene of a shooting in nearby Gommern. Captain Breman was notified by informants of a blond haired man answering the description of Mannraptor staying at the Gildenhouser Inn in Gommern. The Inn was surrounded by Captain Breman, Special Agent Lawrence Dunnington and twelve local Polazi Officers. When one of the Polazi officers saw the suspect enter a small storage shed he over-reacted and fired into it. At least five of the Polazi officers were armed with Heckler & Koch MP-5 sub-machine gun variants. Two were equipped with fifty-six round drum magazines. The initial overreaction by the Polazi officer started a maelstrom of fire. Dunnington estimates that well over two-hundred rounds penetrated the storage shed. A form was seen fleeing after bursting through the rear wall of the structure. Inside, a great deal of blood was recovered. DNA test of the blood have become the source of some contention in Berlin. Samples have been forwarded to various centers for further testing. There seems to be some question as to whether the samples are even human blood. On a personal note; agent Dunnington has an exemplary record. He does not deserve the treatment he is receiving for his defense of Captain Breman. It is my hope that a report to our Director will at least relieve some pressure being put on Lawrence Dunnington for his excellent work.

- Operational Directive, O. I. S. –
(Office of International Security)

RE: To all personnel and Field agents involved in the pursuit of Boris Mannraptor.

Obviously to any thinking person, the Boris Mannraptor case is an extraordinary one. I am re-directing a full analysis wing to our fellow Boris.

It has become plain that we are dealing with more than a serial killer who has a great many international connections. Data Control is at a loss. They seem to have given up on the psychological warfare theory. Now they are not sure where to turn. It seems no one wants to discuss the DNA findings. As Boris Mannraptor has not surfaced since the shooting in Gommern, perhaps this ordeal will end. Until then all personnel and agents are directed to use extreme caution in following any new leads. There must be absolute silence in the face of questions dealing with this case. Near panic has broken out in Berlin because of a leak after the first report on the DNA was released. They have recovered several more bodies in the Gommern area. Rumors are breaking out that these victims were killed after the Gommern shooting incident ...

Is Christianity Logical?

Expressions, 2003

It has been said that if there were not a God, man would create one. Obviously, this is true because of the many different religions in the world today. Every culture in recorded history has had religious beliefs and customs. These religious beliefs were closely tied to that particular culture's explanation of the origins of life. It stands to reason, as drastically different as man's religions are, they all cannot be right.

As religion always involves elements of the supernatural, any religious belief must be accepted with a degree of blind faith. Some religions are so fanciful as to be beyond the realm of acceptance by the modern, educated mind. Is there any religion that can be somehow tested? What criteria could one use to test the merits of any religion? Difficult questions, but surprisingly history and science both offer evidence for Christianity being a logical faith.

If the Christian Bible were checked for historical accuracy, the first thing a study would show is how close chronologically the authors were to the events recorded. According to William Albright, one of the world's foremost Biblical archaeologists, "There is no longer any reason to date any of the New Testament beyond A.D.'50 to A.D.'75." Another leading Biblical archaeologist, Doctor John A. T. Robinson concludes that the entire New Testament was written before the fall of Jerusalem in A.D.'70. By comparison, the Gathas of Zoroaster (about 1,000 B.C.) were not put into writing until after the third century. The most popular Parsi biography of Zoroaster was written in A.D.1278.

The Buddha, who lived in the sixth century B.C., produced no written scriptures. It was not until the late part of the first century A.D. that his biography was written.

The sayings of Muhammad, who lived from 570 to 632 A.D. are recorded in the Koran. However, his biography was not written until the year 767, more than a century after his death.

By comparison, the Christian Bible's historical accuracy is much more likely to be assured. If compared to other works of antiquity, the chronological gap widens even more. Thucydides wrote his history in 460 to 400 B.C., yet all that exists are eight manuscripts written about 900 A.D. – almost thirteen hundred years after he wrote.

The writings of Herodotus are also very few and were written over thirteen hundred years after his original writings. Classical historian F. F. Bruce concludes, "No classical scholar would listen to an argument that the authenticity of Herodotus or Thucydides is in question because their works are over thirteen hundred years older than the originals."

Aristotle wrote his Poetics around 343 B.C. The earliest extant copy is dated A.D. 1100; nearly fourteen hundred years after he wrote, and only five manuscripts remain.

Caesar's history of the Gaelic wars of 58 and 50 B.C. is passed down to us in only nine copies dating one thousand years after his death.

If the few, and old manuscripts listed here are considered authentic by the experts, what are we to make of the mountains of New Testament manuscripts passed down to us?

The "Uncial Manuscripts," written in all Greek capital letters, number three hundred and six. A new style of writing emerged about A.D. 800 called miniscule. We have 2,856 of these manuscripts. There are eight to ten thousand Latin Vulgate manuscripts and eight thousand Ethiopic, Slavic and Armenian. In all, there are more than 24,000 New Testament manuscripts in existence dating to within a generation of the event that founded Christianity. There is no contest in manuscript authority in either chronological proximity, or volume of work.

But, what other sources might exist to bolster a logical belief in the Christian Bible? Josephus, a first century historian born in A.D. 37, mentions Jesus, His trial and His crucifixion. He also confirms many other details in his official writings. The Roman historian Tacitus' writing in A.D. 115 explicitly mentions the persecutions of the Christians in A.D. 64. He places Christ, His trial, and Pontius Pilatus all in proper historical perspective. There exists a large collection of letters written by Pliny the Younger to his friend, the Emperor Tragen that has been preserved. In these writings he describes the brutal interrogation of a new sect called "Christians."

Thallus, who in A.D. 52 wrote a history of the Eastern Mediterranean, is quoted by Julius Africanus in A.D. 221. It seems Thallus wrote of an unusual solar eclipse in A.D. 33. The Greek author and historian Phlegon writes that in the fourth year of the 202nd Olympiad (i.e. 33 A.D.) "There was a great eclipse of the sun." He reports that this eclipse was experienced in Rome, Athens, and other Mediterranean cities. This phenomenon is also confirmed by Roman writer and historian Tertullian. Their records coincide with the New Testament account of darkness at the hour of Christ's death.

As extensive as this historical record is, it has from time to time, fallen under fire from critics. The accuracy of John, Luke, Mark, Josephus, and others are called into question. Yet archaeology has vindicated many of these writers. Archaeology has proven the five porticoes of the pool of Bethesda as described in John 5:1 – 15. For years critics used this as an example of New Testament inaccuracies – until it was discovered under forty feet of earth. Also confirmed was the pool of Siloam (John 9:7), Jacob's well (John 9:12), and the stone pavement near the Joppa Gate where Jesus was said to appear before Pilate (John 9:3), as well as Pilate's identity.

Josephus' description of Herod's harbor at Caesarea was considered wrong for years. Then under-water discoveries proved that Josephus was accurately describing the harbor of his day.

Archaeology has proven Luke correct in his naming of Lysanias as Tetrarch of Abila (AD. 14 to 37), long thought to be wrong. He also accurately described thirty-two countries, fifty-four cities, and nine islands.

Archaeologists have also proven an order given by Cauis Vibruis Maximus, Prefect of Egypt, for people to return to their original provinces for the census. The existence and locations of Nazareth and Jericho have also been confirmed.

Conclusion ...

When Jesus gave the two great commandments recorded in Mark 12:30, the instructions were clear, to love God with all your heart, soul, and mind. In considering that no other major religion has such historical or archaeological evidence behind it, one may wonder if the "mind" was mentioned in the great commandment for obvious reasons.

Albright, William;   Recent Discoveries in Bible Lands

Bruce, F. F.;   The New Testament Documents:

Are they Reliable?

Free, Joseph;   Archaeology and Bible History

Schaff, Philip;   History of the Christian Church

Strobel, Lee;   The Case for Christ

Oh, Israel

Expressions, 2003

Child of Israel, do not mourn
For the martyrs that have died,
Or for the temple, still in ruins
For your God is at your side.

You have suffered persecution
And have been scattered through the lands,
Your men have fallen by the sword,
But still your nation stands.

In the past you have gone astray
And failed to hear God's call,
So He let you come to hardship
And He let your cities fall.

Your history ... long and bloody
And your people, for so long pained,
But your God has not forgotten you,
As your homeland stands regained.

For God will keep His promises
Your people's cries are not ignored,
The temple soon to be rebuilt,
Oh, Israel ... your glory restored!

(Dedicated to all God's Children, both Jew and Gentile . . .)

Sand Storm

Expressions, 2003

Winds of change blow shifting sands,
Another cheek will not be turned;
Justice now makes her demands,
Collect rewards so rightly earned.

Life attacked, the righteous scorned,
God profaned and truth betrayed;
So many souls yet to be mourned,
And awesome debts to be repaid.

History will record their shame,
And the vastness of their lie;
How they have tainted Allah's name,
And their cowardice as they die.

The winds of change will blow today,
Blood now stains these ancient sands;
God sees His children led astray,
With weapons grasped in dying hands.

Human kindness coldly spurned,
And so this sand-storm rages;
Again the lesson is not learned,
More blood spilled on history's pages ...

Venus Mons

Expressions, 2003

Venus Mons, in lace and cotton
My love she does demand
The softness of this velvet mound
That now lies beneath my hand

Fingers now inside the fabric
As you part your legs for me
I feel the heat of Venus Mons
And your need is plain to see

I feel her beautiful wetness
That cannot be held inside
This cotton and lace so wet with want
From your needs too long denied

And as I touch this velvet mound
And she is thrust into the air
My want to taste her glistening lips
Become more then I can bear

I remove your wetted garment
And I see the want in you
I am now consumed with hunger
And you know what I must do

I hear you crying out now
As you writhe against my face
Venus Mons and I are one
As we lock in loves embrace ...

Chapter 8

Hail Gladius

Honorable Mention – Expressions, 2002

Hail Gladius, I salute you Caesar
As you let the games begin
I hold this symbol of the sport
To cut down the legs of men

For Caesar, we will play this game
And for Caesar, we will kill
Blood does entertain our emperor ...
So I wield this length of steel

Blades will clash for the roaring crowd
A kill is what they need
I see my opponent growing weak
This human soon to bleed

I see his weakness, an opening ...
Now I will put this man to rest
Gladius ... my blade of thirsty steel
Now deep within his chest

A sudden gasp, I see his pain
A twist of blade assures my win
But all his death will mean to me ...
I will live to perform again

The games continue, lives will pass
And the time has come for me
I feel the coldness of the steel
Hail Gladius ... set me free.

Empty Chairs

Honorable Mention – Expressions, 2002

Empty chairs and empty lives,
Empty tokens held as dear;
A hollow gesture made in vain,
By a people gripped with fear.

These empty chairs, like empty words,
Still echo in our ears;
Do they have the ring of reason?
Or do they play upon our fears?

"Such an eyesore, quickly ...
Its presence makes us weep!"
The rubble that could show the truth,
Carted off and buried deep.

So many questions still unasked,
It seems that no one dares;
The crime scene now paved over,
And in its place ... these empty chairs.

Other voices cry out loudly,
That perhaps ... we are deceived;
Each one silenced in his turn,
Can these accusers be believed?

Do the spirits now bear witness?

From this monument we have laid?
Have they found peace in watching?
The weakness we've displayed?

Are the victims really honored?
By tears and empty stares?
We must be brave and find the truth,
Give meaning to these chairs ...

The Small Green Tree Lizard

Expressions, 2002

As time passes, I only miss you more. The farther away you go, the closer I feel to you.

I can no longer deny I love you ... my denial has become such a farce, that for me to even think it, is a poignant reminder of how hopeless my case is.

Completely lost to me now, you continue to haunt my existence.

As I feel the wind on my face, I see it in your hair. That beautiful raven hair that is surely graying by now. . Graying, as mine is, as this time passes. As time passes ... without you.

I have robbed myself of the wondrous pleasure of growing old with you.

My aging is no longer a mark of how long I have lived, but a mark of how long I have been without you.

At night I look skyward to the stars. I stand alone under them and wonder ... Can you see these same stars? ...

I see them twinkle, as your eyes used to twinkle. I feel the tears on my face now, as I saw them on your face so many times before.

The pain I so callously inflicted on your poor troubled being, now hammers at my wretched consciousness reducing me to ash ...

Like the ash of the leaf piles you used to burn, as you tirelessly tended our yard.

The autumn leaves torment me as they fall, each one mocking my loss.

The clouds overhead come from nowhere as does your image ... then disappears just as quickly.

I cannot escape your memory ... do I want to ... or do I revel in the sadness it causes me? ...

I see the birds, the squirrels, the small green tree lizard at the corner of the house, they are asking me ... where is she?

These creatures that you so loved ask things of me I cannot answer ... where is she?

Is there no mercy for me even in nature? Do the pine trees we planted together, that have grown so tall ... do they hold me responsible as well?

I hear a ringing in the distance ... could it be a phone? Could this be a call for me? A call from you asking me to come home? ... Yes, one last call, please ... it is only the ringing in my ears ... The ringing that now haunts me, an empty ringing from the past.

The years, so many ... stacked one on top of the other, like the brick I laid.

Twenty-two of them ... twenty-two, like the MKII you were so good with ...

How I long to be the beer bottle that sits down range ... waiting for you to squeeze off another round.

But not to be ... I must live my days and my night as well.

The days I move forward to where I go, the nights, back to where I was.

This strange passage through time only makes my memory sharper and sharper.

Were my memories a blade, I could easily use it to slash my wrist ... to try and escape as Sylvia did ...

Is there nothing I can say that does not evoke your memory? ... I think not.

If only this void within me could be filled in as easily as the cellar I dug.

I stand speechless ... and the small green tree lizard scurries away without an answer

Finis

Printed in the United States
By Bookmasters

Printed in the United States
By Bookmasters